# A Killing In D.C.

# The Chronicles of Detective Marcus Rose

## By

# A.D. White

A.D. White

www.adwhite.net

ISBN-13:978-1499660463
ISBN-10:1499660464

A.D. White

**www.adwhite.net**

# <u>Acknowledgements</u>

Thanks to my wonderful family for supporting me and encouraging me to follow my dream.

All characters are the work of the author's imagination.  This book is a work of fiction and not meant to depict real life events.

**Cover Art Designed by Colette Butfiloski**

A.D. White

**www.adwhite.net**

# CHAPTERS

# Chapter One
# Detective Marcus Rose

As the buzzer to the alarm clock sounded, Marcus looked over at the clock in disgust before silencing it. Four thirty in the morning. "Damn, this is too early for human beings to get up," he thought to himself. Marcus had worked his share of dayshifts on the police department and after twenty years he still wasn't used to getting up at this time. Monday mornings were bad enough but getting up at the ass crack of dawn only made it worse.

His wife Gina was sound asleep. The alarm didn't seem to bother her though. He slowly rose from the bed and opened up the middle drawer of his night stand to retrieve his service weapon, then walked slowly through the dark to the bathroom to get dressed. Gina didn't have to get up for another hour.

Every night he laid out his clothes in the bathroom so he didn't have to turn on any lights in the bedroom and wake her. He went through his normal ritual of the three S's. Shit, shower and shave is what they called it many years ago when he was in the military. He walked out of the bathroom fully dressed in his suit and tie but with his shoes in hand. Gina didn't like shoes worn in their house. She said shoes distributed nasty germs all around the house so Marcus abided by her wishes. You know what they say "Happy wife, happy life." As he quietly walked through the bedroom, his cell phone rang, loudly. "Damn Marcus" moaned Gina as he walked out of the bedroom while answering the phone.

"Detective Rose, uh-huh, really, Georgetown, greeaat" was his sarcastic response to the voice on the other end that told him there had been an apparent suicide and he was on the bubble. Marcus was a Detective First Grade on the D.C. Police Department. He had been assigned to the Homicide Division for the last eight years. Homicide investigated all deaths, even suicides.

He was thought to be one of the best detectives not just in homicide, but on the entire police department. Marcus was a member of squad 1, which included four other detectives. All of whom received the same phone call as Marcus, but they didn't have to respond to the location unless the lead detective needed their assistance. Marcus was on the bubble, meaning that he would be the lead detective in this particular investigation. The other detectives in his squad would assist in tracking leads as needed.

Before Marcus headed out of the front door, he walked back into the bedroom and kissed Gina on the cheek as she lay there half asleep. "Goodbye babe, I'm gone. Got a scene up in Georgetown that I gotta go to." Gina's eyes opened, "you be careful, okay." "Okay babe," Marcus responded, "talk to you later" as he bent down and kissed her on her exposed thigh. Gina smiled "don't start nothin you can't finish detective." "I can finish it, don't make me prove it" (as he jokingly tugged at his belt buckle). "Yeah right, I think it would be best for everyone involved if you went and solved that crime waiting for you, Mr. Detective," she jokingly responded. "You know I love you though" she said with a smile and rolled over. "Uhm, uhm, you just be ready when I get home. Daddy needs some lovin girl," he chuckled. Marcus and Gina had been married for twenty one years, even before Marcus joined the police department. She had stuck with him through thick and thin. Things were fine now, but it hadn't always been that way.

Being a police officer can take a toll on a marriage. The long hours, court appearances and special events took Marcus away from home for too many hours out of the day and most weekends, making Gina feel like she was a single parent to their two boys. Gina had no idea what she was getting herself into when they met twenty-three years ago. He was a cop in the Air Force and stationed in North Carolina. Gina worked at the Base Exchange. They both were a lot younger and thinner back then.

Marcus was on patrol one fine day when he came upon a motorist with a flat tire. He activated his lights and pulled over to help. He saw a slim, light skinned woman with short brown hair. She was very pretty and oozed sex appeal. There she stood, holding a jack in one hand and a lug wrench in the other. She was looking at them as if they were something that she had never seen before. "Do you know what to do with those" Marcus jokingly asked. "Of course I do" she responded. "Okay, what's this for" as he took the jack out of her hand? "It's a jack thingy, you know to...jack the car" said Gina. "And this" he asked while taking the lug wrench out of her other hand? "It's for hitting you up side your head if you don't help me" she joked. "I got you" Marcus responded. "I'm here to serve, protect and change the flat tires of pretty women" he said with a devilish grin.

"Umh, don't tell me that you're a player Airman (as she looked at his name tag) Rose". "No ma'am, I'm no player, just a hard working man coming to the rescue of a damsel in distress. My name is Marcus" as he put the jack on the ground and held out his hand. "I'm Gina" as she met his hand with hers. "I've seen you working at the Base Exchange" said Marcus. "Really" she responded. "I've never noticed you there" she said with a grin. Actually, she had seen Marcus in the store and she liked what she saw. She wanted to talk to him but wasn't the type of woman to make the first move. She took this as fate intervening. "Well, give me a couple of minutes and I'll have this tire changed for you, then you can go home to your husband" Marcus said inquisitively. "No husband" she responded. "Boyfriend" he asked. "No...no boyfriend".

After Marcus changed the tire he looked at Gina and said "Well, it was a pleasure meeting you Gina. Maybe next time I see you it won't be on the side of the road". Gina laughed "oh, you trying to insinuate something there, Airman Rose"? "No ma'am" said Marcus as he glared into her eyes. "Let me pay you for your road side assistance" Gina said as she reached for her purse, knowing full well that he would not accept any money.

"Oh no" said Marcus. "I have a much better idea. Go to lunch with me?" She looked at Marcus and responded jokingly "I don't have to worry about stranger danger with you, do I?" "No ma'am, you don't. I'm Officer Friendly" as he smiled. "Okay, I'll go out with you if you promise to stop calling me ma'am". "Okay Gina" what's your number (as he took out his notebook); I'll give you a call." They bonded quickly and became friends, then lovers. Two years later, they married and she followed him back to his hometown of Washington, D.C., when he was honorably discharged.

Marcus joined the police academy two weeks after leaving the military, while Gina attended nursing school. After the academy, Marcus walked a beat in the Trinidad section of northeast, D.C. Gina eventually got a job at one of the local hospitals. They were a successful couple in the making, except, they rarely saw each other. Gina worked during the morning hours but Marcus' shift rotated every two weeks. They were like two ships passing in the day and sometimes in the night. Between working, going to court and choir practice after work with his fellow officers, Marcus was never at home. Drinking with his friends after work was coined "choir practice". He'd come home wound up and smelling like alcohol. He spent his days chasing bad guys and fighting crime and he needed time to wind down. What more did she want from him, he wondered?

Gina complained about his absence but it didn't seem to be getting through to Marcus. It was a hazard of the job and something that facilitated the ending of many marriages among his peers. Gina was lonely and when she started hanging out with her co-workers, that got Marcus' attention. He knew when Gina became pregnant with their first child, things had to change. Her parents were still together and she had a strong sense of family. When Gina said "I do" and *"till death do us part"* she meant it.

One night, Marcus came home at two in the morning to find Gina's bags packed and sitting in the living room. She explained to him that if she had to raise this child with an absent father, she might as well be living on her own. Gina had no intention of leaving but she knew she needed to get his attention. Marcus was a good man. Young and a little immature but he too had a sense of family and wasn't one to shirk his responsibilities. There's one sure thing about having a child, it will either make you or break you. It will either expose a man's weaknesses' and shortcomings or propel him into manhood. When his first son was born Marcus quickly grew up and took on all his responsibilities as a father and husband. Gina never had to scare him like that again.

# Chapter Two
# The Crime Scene

As Marcus drove through the Cleveland Park neighborhood of Georgetown he couldn't help but notice how clean it was. A warm and sunny day. Blue skies littered with white cumulus clouds resembling children joyfully playing in the skies. Green blossoming trees with colorful flowers throughout many of the front yards. An affluent part of town that was no stranger to crime, but violent crimes were not commonplace.

Marcus pulled onto 36th street and parked. He noticed that the home was large and stately. "They must have a lot of money. This has to be worth at least a two mil, he thought to himself." He could see the police cars in front of the residence with lights flashing. Two officers standing at the front door securing the scene. "Officers, how ya doing today" he asked, as he approached opening the left side of his suit jacket, exposing his badge. "Detective" responded one of the officers as he nodded to Marcus and stepped aside allowing him entry into the home.

As he entered, he stopped just inside the front door, reached into his inside jacket pocket and removed his notebook. He stood there, surveying the home and documenting his observations in his notebook. This was his ritual for every potential crime scene that he responded to. His detailed notes often helped him later in his investigations. Never trust every detail to memory is what he was taught.   As time passed, memories changed but what was written in his notebook remained the same.  A formal dining room to the left and the living room to his right.  He made note that everything looked neat and appeared to be in order.   Of course, he wouldn't know that for sure until he talked to someone familiar with the home.

"Hey Marcus, glad you could join us" barked Detective Logan Steele.  Detective Steele was Marcus' partner.  He was new to the homicide unit and Marcus was mentoring him in murder investigations.  Logan was a seventeen year veteran of the police department and had spent the last five years in the Narcotics Division. He was great at his job, but that had consisted of buying drugs off the street and conducting investigations into mid-level drug dealers in D.C.  Investigating murders was new to him and he was learning from the best.

"Good morning to you Steele.  Did you pick up my coffee on the way" asked Marcus?   "You know I'm a detective not a gopher" replied Logan.  Marcus clenched his lips and gave Logan a look.  Marcus had a way of looking at people that could tell exactly what he was thinking.  I guess you could say that it was written all over his face.  "It's in the car" replied Logan.  "Thanks. What do we have here" asked Marcus.

As Detective Steele glanced at his notebook. "We've got a white female lying on the kitchen floor, to the left of the center island. Gun shot wound to her left temple. Blood spatter on the top of the island. A gun lying to the right of her and a suicide note on the kitchen counter."

They both walked to the kitchen and stopped just inside the doorway. "Who found the body," asked Marcus? "The house keeper. She entered the house with her own key around four am, said the alarm was on and the front door was locked. Started cleaning up and didn't notice the body until she got to the kitchen". "Where's she now?" "She's in the maid's quarters waiting to be questioned" said Logan. "Maid's quarters" Marcus said surprisingly. "Must be nice" he said sarcastically.

"Is crime scene finished processing" asked Marcus. "Yeah, they finished up a few minutes ago. Waiting on you to do your thing then the Medical Examiner (M.E.) can move the body". "You got an I.D. on her yet" asked Marcus. "Yeah, her name is Laura Whittington. She's twenty five years old and lives here alone. Her father is Robert Whittington". "Why do I know that name" Marcus inquired. "Because he's the same Robert Whittington that owns Whittington Pharmaceuticals. Extremely wealthy and a bit of a shark. Pisses off a lot of people with his business deals and he's been buying up the city for the last few years." "Wow...he's not gonna be happy, huh", Marcus said with a smirk.

Marcus observed Laura Whittington lying on the floor, face up in a pool of blood and dressed in a black negligee. Marcus glanced over at a picture of the victim on the refrigerator door "she was a real looker huh" said Marcus. "Yeah, that's putting it lightly. She was fine as hell" said Logan. "Okay Fido, calm down. Have a little respect for the dead" said Marcus with a little chuckle. "Where's the note?" "On the counter Sherlock" replied Logan, pointing to the note." Marcus looked at the note, then back at the body. Looked at the note again, then walked back to the body, bent over and visually examined her face. "Hmmm, interesting" as he played with the hairs of his goatee. "Okay Steele, tell me what you see here". "Well, looks like a suicide to me. Gun on the floor, crime scene swabbed her hands, so we'll see if she has any gun shot residue on them. Suicide note on the counter. Everything looks in order, no signs of any kind of struggle. All the doors were locked and no signs of forced entry. Looks clear cut to me" Logan said prideful like, as to pat himself on the back.

Marcus shook his head no and walked out of the kitchen. Logan just stood there looking confused. Marcus came back a couple of minutes later. "Grass Hopper, you've got a lot to learn" said Marcus. "This is a homicide, she's been murdered". "How do you figure that?" Logan asked. "First of all, she was shot in the left temple which would indicate that she shot herself with the gun in her left hand. She's right handed and it's kinda hard to shoot yourself in the left temple with your right hand." "How do you know that she's right handed?" asked Logan. "I asked the maid" replied Marcus.

"Also, if she shot herself with her left hand, why is the gun on the right side of her body? Marcus looked at Logan but got no response. Did you notice the slight bruising around her neck? Looks like someone choked her before shooting her. Look at her eyes" as Marcus bent over the body and pointed. Logan walked over and looked. "Do you see those red spots?" asked Marcus. "Yeah" replied Logan. "That's called petechial hemorrhaging and that occurs due to a lack of oxygen when someone is asphyxiated. Logan stood there looking dumbfounded. And the suicide note, it's typed. Who in the heck types a suicide note? Not to mention that it's not signed. "Call the rest of the squad; we've got a murder to solve".

A.D. White

# Chapter Three
# Meet the Squad

*Detective Second Grade Logan Steele* was Marcus' partner and trainee. He was six feet five inches in height with a shaved head and mustache. Logan had an athletic build and was a fitness buff. He had a commanding presence and loved to work out and play basketball. Oh yeah, and he had an appetite for the women. A real ladies man, chased anything in a skirt which sometimes clouded his judgment. He was streetwise with a sarcastic sense of humor. His sense of humor helped him bond with Marcus, because he too had a sarcastic tone to his humor. Logan had street smarts but was very impatient. He grew up in the streets of Brooklyn, New York, where at an early age he gained a reputation as a fighter. His childhood nickname was "Slugger". He moved to D.C., to attend Howard University on a sports scholarship and remained there after he graduated. Logan called the rest of the squad and informed them that this was a homicide and that they needed to respond to the crime scene.

The first to arrive was *Detective Second Grade Katelyn Alverez* whose nickname was "Al". She works harder than everyone else because she feels like she has something to prove since she's female and a minority. It doesn't help that her father is a retired D.C., police officer who always wanted a boy to follow in his footsteps, but had four daughters. Being the oldest of his children she wants to live up to his expectations and she can't do that being a prissy girl. Some people on the department have openly questioned if she got her Detective's shield to fill a quota which only made her more determined to prove them wrong. She is twenty-eight years old, five feet five with an hour glass figure, sexy and tough. Long black hair that she keeps pinned up. Steele often comments that she has an ass like J-Lo. She's been on the department for seven years and in homicide for one year.

The next to arrive was *Detective Second Grade Anthony Russo* who most people referred to as "Big Russ". He is "Mr. Intelligence" who analyzes everything. He's a numbers guy and always quotes statistics. Way too serious with no sense of humor. Short, round and balding on top. He's been on the police department for thirty years and a homicide detective for fifteen years. Has seen every type of murder scene over the span of his career and was desensitized to it all long ago, but lately has been regaining his humanity and starting to show the affects of what he's seen over the years.

Once arriving at the crime scene, each member walked gently around the house looking for any clues. They all took notes which would be used in their after crime scene meeting. Logan and Al were both in the kitchen. "Al, come here and look at this" Logan said pointing to the victims eyes. "See the spots, that's called petechial hemorrhaging, indicating that the victim may have been asphyxiated". Al looked at Logan with disgust "no shit Sherlock, that's basic Homicide 101. Marcus probably just told you that". "Pssss" as Logan blew air from his lips, "I knew that before Marcus even got here." "Pssss, whatever" was her response. Al walked away shaking her head and as always, Logan watched her walk away. Let's just say, he liked the view. After each member finished gathering information from the crime scene, they all met in the living room.

During the meeting *Detective Second Grade Raymond Barlow* was the last member of the squad arrived on scene. He went by the nickname, Ray. He was tall, at six feet three, handsome with a slim build. Ray was also a ladies man and chases as many women as he can, which is one of his weaknesses. His reputation with the ladies is well known throughout the department. He was a classmate of Detective Steele in the police academy and they play basketball together on occasion. Ray is impulsive and often acts before he thinks things out. He's been a homicide detective for four years.

"Okay, the M.E.'s about to take the body; is there anything else you need from the scene?" Marcus asked. They all shook their heads no. "The maid said that the front door was locked when she arrived and the security alarm was on". Detective Alverez added "all the downstairs windows were locked when I checked, not sure about upstairs". "Okay, I'll check the upstairs windows. How the suspect left the house is my next question. He would have needed a key to lock the front door behind him...but he could have exited through an upstairs window" said Marcus.

"The upstairs windows are alarmed too, so he couldn't have left through any of those" said Detective Barlow. "Okay, Russ and Logan do a canvass of all the houses on both sides of this block. Find out if anyone heard or saw anything that we might be able to use. Also find out what they know about the victim. I'm sure there's a nosey neighbor or two somewhere around here. Al and Ray check the block behind this house for the same. It's nine a.m., now, let's all meet back at the squad room at eleven thirty." "Okay" said Ray, c'mon Katie let's go." "How many times do I have to tell you not to call me Katie? My name is Al or Alverez to you", she responded. "My bad, let's go Kate" he said with a shit eating grin as they both walked out.

At eleven thirty they were all back at the squad room for their meeting. Detectives from the other squads sat in there also, so the room was rather large. On this particular week, squad two was working the evening shift and squad three was working the midnight shift. Since Marcus was the lead detective on this investigation, he was in charge of the meeting.

Each squad has a sergeant who supervises the detectives. Sergeant Ulysses Gant is squad one's sergeant. They referred to him as Sergeant U or just Sarge. Sergeant U walked out of his office which was adjacent to the squad room. "Okay, what you got" he asked Marcus? "The victims name is Laura Whittington and she is the daughter of the very wealthy Robert Whittington. She was found on the kitchen floor by the maid a little after four a.m., with what appeared to the untrained eye to be a self inflicted gun shot wound to the left temple, as he glanced at Logan.

Further examination of the body shows slight bruising on the neck and hemorrhaging in the eyes indicating that she may have been strangled before she was shot. There was a typed and unsigned suicide note on the kitchen counter that read "I love you mom and dad. I'm sorry". Apparently, someone wants us to think that she killed herself."

What else do we know" asked Sergeant U? Detective Steele chimed in "I talked to the next door neighbor" looking at his notebook "whose name is Ms. Craig. She states that Laura Whittington has a steady boyfriend named Walter, but that she's also seen another man coming and going. Detective Barlow chimed in, "I talked to the neighbor who lives directly behind the victim's house and she noticed a tall black male walking in the alley this morning about three a.m., wearing dark clothes. She couldn't see his face and couldn't give me a better description."

"I also talked to the maid. She came in and cleaned half of the first floor before she noticed the body in the kitchen. She could have totally contaminated the crime scene before we got there" added Ray. "Good point" said Sergeant U. "Looking at Detective Alverez, Sergeant U asked "do you have anything to add?" No Sarge, everyone that I talked to didn't see or hear anything and they really didn't know much about the victim except who her father was".

Detective Russo jumped in "the neighbor I talked to says that the boyfriend drives a red sports car with personalized tags of "Walt". I ran the tags and they come back to Walter Chase of Bethesda, Maryland. Odds are that he's our man, Sarge". Sergeant U knew that if he asked Detective Russo why he thought that, he would get all kinds of statistics and that this would irritate the other detectives, who had grown tired of hearing him spout statistics.

"Detective Russo, why do you think that the boyfriend is the perpetrator of this crime" he asked with a sly grin? As Detective Russo stood up, the other detectives slumped in their seats and groaned. "Twenty three percent of all murder victims are female and one third of those victims were killed by their intimate partners". "Okay, we get it" interrupted Detective Barlow. "The spouse or the boyfriend is always a prime suspect. Katelyn and I will track down the boyfriend and have him come in for questioning". As everyone looked at Detective Alverez, she started to say "If you call me

Katelyn one more time" then she was interrupted by Lieutenant O'Malley yelling at the top of his lungs "Rose, Steele, my office...NOW!"

Lieutenant O'Malley was in charge of all the homicide detectives. He directly supervised the sergeants, who directly supervised the detectives. He was referred to by the detectives as Lieutenant or Lieu, for short. O'Malley was not only overweight, but he had diabetes and high blood pressure as well. He always seemed to be in a bad mood and no one wanted to be called into his office. It's like being called into the Principal's office. Most of the time it's not going be a pleasant visit.

Although you couldn't tell it, he liked and respected Marcus because Marcus solved cases and in the long run that's all that really mattered. Now how he felt about Logan Steele was a different story. He saw Logan as a smart ass and someone that didn't respect authority and needless to say, that didn't sit well with him. "Close the door behind you" he said as Marcus, Logan and Sergeant U entered his office. "It's only been a few hours and I've already got the Chief of Police crawling up my ass about this case. Do you have any suspects?" "Not yet sir, still going over everything" said Marcus. "This is going to be a high profile case and you're the lead on this one. Everything has to be done by the numbers and I need an arrest on this like yesterday" said Lieutenant O'Malley.

"We got this Lieu" said Logan. O'Malley looked at Logan with disgust and said "the only reason that you're in here is to learn from Marcus. I'll tell you when I want you to speak, otherwise, look, listen and learn". Logan nodded his head in silence. "I want daily updates on this case; now close the door behind you." As all three started to walk out, the lieutenant said "I've got my eye on you Steele". Logan mumbled, "that's the same thing his wife said". "What did you say Steele," yelled the lieutenant? Sergeant U pushed Logan out of the door and closed it behind them. "You like to live dangerously don't you Steele" said Sergeant U as he shook his head. "You know the lieutenant is never in a good mood and all you do is piss him off more, then he crawls up my ass.

Shit rolls down hill Steele, remember that! If he makes my life miserable I'm gonna do the same for you! Logan looked at Sergeant U and said "I don't see you solving any cases". Marcus cringed as he knew what was coming next. "Listen Detective" said Sergeant U, "it's not my job to solve cases. It's my job to make sure that YOU solve cases. It's called supervision and when done properly it may appear that I am doing little or nothing at all". Logan looked away and asked "so when I see you doing nothing, you're actually doing your job?" "EXACTLY and don't ever question me again...Detective...or I'll have your ass walking a foot beat along the Potomac River. So go do some damn detecting...Detective!"

# Chapter Four
## Sorry For Your Loss

Detective Russo was tasked by Sergeant U to notify the family of Laura Whittington of her death. This is always a delicate situation and you need the right amount of compassion as well as professionalism. Big Russ has done this for years and in the past this would have been no big deal for him.

But lately, death and its collateral damage had been getting the best of him. Homicide detectives quickly learn how to insulate themselves from the emotions that most of us feel surrounding death. If they allowed themselves to feel, the sight of all the dead bodies and the horrid stories that accompanied them, it would eventually eat them up inside, rendering them ineffective. Emotions prevent clear thought, thus, making their job difficult, if not impossible. Lately, he has been unable to completely detach himself from this process. In the past, the job had made him numb, but much to his dismay, he was starting to feel again.

Russo took the long drive out to Potomac, Maryland, to notify the family. It was nice to get out of the city for once. He enjoyed the suburban scenery. The green grass and tree lined streets. It's not like D.C., didn't have any grass and trees, it did, but most of it was like a concrete jungle and sometimes he just needed to get away. The atmosphere just seemed different out in the burbs. As he drove around the beltway, he purposely filled his head with pleasant thoughts, trying not to think about the task at hand.

Big Russ pulled up to the gated community and was greeted by a security guard. "Can I help you sir," asked the guard? "Yes, my name is Detective Russo from the D.C. Police Department. I'm looking for the Whittington residence. Can you point me in the right direction?" "Sure, are they expecting you," he asked? "Ah, no. No they're not," he replied. "Okay, I'm gonna have to give them a call first. Standby please," said the guard as he walked back into his shack and picked up the telephone. After a couple of minutes, the guard walked back out and said "go down to the second corner and make a right turn" as he pointed down the street. "The Whittington residence will be the second house on the left. They are now expecting you sir." Big Russ drove down the street and pulled into the large circular driveway of the Whittington residence.

As he parked, the large double doors of the house opened and there stood a lady in her fifties, neatly dressed in a grey skirt and a white button up shirt. Salt and pepper hair, attractive and classy looking. With the exception of being much older, a carbon copy of the victim. Big Russ assumed correctly that this was the victim's mother. The look on her face was that of fearful curiosity. She wondered why a policeman from

Washington, D.C., would be driving out to Maryland to see her.

As Big Russ walked up the stairs to meet her, she stepped onto the porch and said "hi, I'm Maureen Whittington, is everything alright?" "No ma'am. My name is Detective Russo from the D.C. Police Department and I'm afraid that I have some very bad news for you." Her mouth opened as her jaw dropped waiting in anticipation, fearful of what was next to come. Big Russ cleared his throat as he noticed tears welling up in Maureen Whittington's eyes. "May I come inside ma'am," he asked? Laura Whittington did not respond verbally. She turned around and walked into the house.

Big Russ followed her and closed the door behind them. "Is there anyone else home ma'am," he asked? (When giving death notifications, detectives always wanted someone else present to console and take care of the family member). "No, I'm here alone. Please tell me why you're here," she pleaded. "Is there someone that you can call to come over," he asked? "My husband should be here soon, or is that why you're here? Did something happen to him," she asked as she placed both hands over her mouth in fear?

Just then, Detective Russo's emotions began to emerge. Seeing her tears triggered something inside of him. Tears began to swell up in his eyes when he saw that she was beginning to cry. He tried to fight them back by swallowing hard. As he opened his mouth to speak, he found it difficult to form a sentence. The lump in his throat felt as if it was growing as a tear fell from his eye. He opened his mouth to speak but nothing came out. He was wrestling with his emotions and losing the battle. After all these years on the job and all the deaths that he had seen, why were his emotions coming back at this moment, he thought to himself.

He was beginning to feel overwhelming sympathy for the family members and was no longer able to separate his profession from his feelings. He stopped and paused as he fought back the tears. He took a deep breath in an attempt to regain his composure as he placed his right hand over his mouth and squeezed his lips with his eyes closed. The few seconds of silence that followed seemed like an eternity. As he opened his eyes it appeared that he lost the battle of emotions as tears fell from both his eyes and moisture trickled down from his nostrils.

By his difficulty, Maureen Whittington knew what was to come. She knew that the worst case scenario was being realized and was trapped between wanting to hear his message and not wanting to hear bad news. "Is Laura Whittington your daughter," he tearfully asked? "Yes," she replied as she looked at him now with anger. "Detective, this must be a cruel joke. Don't you dare tell me that something has happened to Laura" as tears rolled down her face. Big Russ gathered his composure for a few seconds "ma'am, I regret to tell you that your daughter Laura was murdered this morning and we will do everything possible to find the person that did it." "No," she shrieked as she crumbled to the floor. She could somehow accept the death of her husband, but not that of her only child.

Big Russ helped her up and walked her over to the couch. "Ma'am, is there someone that I can call for you," he asked? "What happened? How did she..., how did she...die?" "She was shot inside of her home ma'am. Can I call someone for you," again he asked?" Just then, the front door opened and in walked Robert Whittington with a stern look on his face. Maureen Whittington ran to him, "Laura has been killed," she cried. "I know," he angrily replied, "and I will make sure that the police catch the piece of crap that did it." He looked at Big Russ with disgust "detective, you can leave now. I'll get any information that we need from your superiors!" Big Russ looked at Mrs. Whittington and said, "I'm sorry for your loss ma'am."

Big Russ quickly walked out the front door and down the steps to his car. As he drove away, he looked curiously at the Whittington house in his rear view mirror. Relieved that the notification was over but disappointed in himself for not being able to conceal his feelings. "That was unprofessional" is what he kept thinking. He realized that he needed to make a decision. He was fifty one years old and a thirty year veteran of the police department. He was eligible to retire any time that he wanted to and maybe now was the time. He called Sergeant U on his cell phone and said "Sarge, I took care of the notification but I'm gonna need to take leave for the last few hours of my shift." "Are you okay" Sarge replied, "you sound a little funny?" "Yeah, I'm good Sarge. Just need some personal time." "Alright, I'll see you tomorrow Russ."

As Big Russ drove home he felt as if there was a dark cloud over him. It had little to do with the death notification that he had just made and everything to do with the state of his life. Big Russ' wife divorced him five years ago after twenty-five years of marriage and he was lonely. They had no children together and he made the same mistake that many of his peers before him made. The police department was his life and everything revolved around the job. He often went to work early and left late and unfortunately, received little reward. It wasn't all bad. He felt a sense of accomplishment when he helped solve a case and a murderer was sent to prison, but that didn't bring the victim back.

When it was late at night and he was in bed, the job couldn't cuddle up with him. When he was sick and needed a little tender loving care, the job couldn't bring him chicken soup. Sure, he had established friendships on the department during his thirty years and some of them were good friends, but that couldn't take the place of a meaningful relationship with a woman and his friends couldn't always be there in his darkest hours. He had an excellent career but failed to nurture his life outside of the job.

Big Russ stuck his key in the door and stepped inside of his big, beautiful, lonely,  house and began his daily ritual.  He walked to the kitchen to retrieve his bottle of whiskey and a shot glass.  Sat down in his favorite overstuffed chair, removed his weapon from its holster and placed it on the table beside the chair along with the whiskey and shot glass.  He poured himself a drink, raised the glass and looked at it.  He then sat the glass beside his gun.  In his mind, he was deciding which one to use.  After staring at them for a few minutes, he picked up the shot glass and downed the whiskey.  He then poured another drink and sat it beside his gun again.  He stared at his two choices once more and downed the whiskey again.

This went on until he was good and drunk.  Once the bottle was empty he picked up his gun and placed it in his lap.  He stared into space and wondered where his life had taken a wrong turn.  He also wondered what his life would be like once he finally retired and what he had to look forward to.  The fact that he had no life outside of the job is what kept him from retiring.  He was married to his job and couldn't stand the thought of losing the only thing that he had left.  He fell asleep in his favorite chair and didn't awake until the morning. Big Russ had survived one more day.  He showered, shaved, dressed and started another day as Detective Anthony Russo.

# Chapter Five
# Roll Call

Zero six hundred hours and roll call is being held in the detectives' squad room by Sergeant U. "Detective Rose" he calls out. "Here Sarge," Rose responds. "Detective Steele." "Present," Steele responds. "Detective Alverez" as he looks up. "Aqui," she responds as she does every morning. "Detective Russo" he calls out. "Here sir," Big Russ responds. "And last but not least, Detective Barlow". "Here Sarge," Ray responds, while coming through the squad room door.

"Hard night Ray" Sergeant U jokingly asks as he notices that Ray is coming through the door half dressed. He's wearing dress pants and a white t-shirt. His button up dress shirt is draped over his left arm and his jacket and tie are lying on his desk from the day before. Sergeant U laughs and says, "you know, getting dressed at home is the normal procedure for the rest of us." "Who says that I'm coming from home" he says with a smile. "Is that where you got those scratches on your arms from," Logan jokes? "Yeah, she was a screamer," responds Ray. "You are so nasty Ray, she was probably screaming to get away from you," says Alverez. All the detectives laugh. Ray has quite a reputation with the ladies and a lot of the younger men on the department envy him.

"Alright, lets address the case at hand," says Sergeant U as he sees Lieutenant O'Malley enter the squad room. "Where are we on this Rose," asks the lieutenant? "The Medical Examiner rushed the autopsy on this one Lieu." Marcus was then interrupted by Logan saying "her daddy must have pulled some strings, huh? I ain't never seen the M.E., work this fast" he joked. "If you got the strings, you might as well pull em," commented Alverez.

Marcus continued, "the cause of death was not the gun shot. She was strangled to death. The M.E., determined that she was already dead when she was shot in the head. The gun shot was an attempt to make it look like a suicide. It looks like the perp came up behind her, placed his right arm around the front of her neck and cut off her air until she was dead. He then shot her in the left temple while holding her up. We know this because the blood spatter was on the top of the island counter and not on the floor. Everything points to the perp being left handed. The perp then placed the gun on the floor in an attempt to make it look like a suicide. The gun found on the scene was registered to Ms. Whittington. We're checking the ballistics just to verify that it is the weapon that she was shot with."

"And let's not forget that feeble attempt at a suicide letter. Typed, but not signed. I'm not falling for the banana in the tail pipe trick," he joked. "Why do you keep saying he," Ray asked? "Isn't it possible that it could have been a woman?" "I really doubt if most women would be strong enough to strangle her from behind while holding her up and shooting her with the other hand. She'd have to be a big bitch," joked Alverez. Big Russ chimed in "the neighbor said that the boyfriend is about six three and muscular. My money is on him as the perp. Statistics say that most murders inside of a home are committed by someone who knows the victim intimately. He's our man," insists Big Russ.

"Marcus, have we located the boyfriend yet," asked the lieutenant? "Yes sir! His name is Walter Chase and he's scheduled to come in tomorrow morning to be interviewed. His lawyer called and set it up." "He's already lawyered up" asked Big Russ? "Told ya, he's our man." "Any drugs in her system" asked the lieutenant? "The tox screen will be back in a couple of days," responded Marcus. "One other thing Lieu, the medical examiner says that it appears that someone tried to remove evidence from under her fingernails, but he didn't get it all. Not sure if there's enough to get any DNA. Also, no gun shot residue was found on her hands or wrists, which verifies that she didn't fire the weapon."

"Good. Have Steele sit in on the interview with you, maybe he can learn something and I'll be in the observation room next door" said Lieutenant O'Malley as he walked out of the squad room and into his office. Steele looks at Marcus and says "I'm getting tired of the lieutenant's smart ass comments. He's always riding my ass and it's getting real old. If we were back in Brooklyn, I'd kick his ass." Sergeant U looks at Steele and says "you always talking bout New York. If New York is so great, then why don't you take your ass back there," as he's walking to his office? "If I went back, your mother might miss me," mumbled Steele. Marcus laughs and shakes his head "man, you gotta chill. Your mouth's gonna bite you in the butt one of these days."

"The maid is coming in to be formally interviewed. She'll be here in about an hour," said Marcus. Sergeant U stops, turns around and says, "Good, I want Alverez to be in on it with you." "Why, because we're both Latino," asks Alverez? "Yep, that's exactly why. You being there will help make her comfortable and will help with any language barriers that might arise," responded Sergeant U. "Okay Sarge" says Alverez. Marcus and Steele walk over to their desks, which face each other.

Logan was frustrated and asked, "how do you keep from losing your cool and telling the bosses exactly what you think of them? I've never even heard you curse before. How the hell do you do it?" Marcus paused before speaking "I have a very good filter. Trust me, I think it but I don't say it. There are times when no one should know what you're thinking. If the bosses knew what I was thinking half of the time, I would have been fired years ago. A person that says that they don't hold their tongue for anybody, is a fool. Be very selective with whom you divulge your thoughts. You have a few more years left before you can retire and you never know when you're gonna need that person. Once you burn a bridge, it's pretty hard to come back across it. I choose to take the high road." "Yeah, I'll try, but it ain't gonna be easy," joked Logan.

"It's not that hard Logan. You gain respect by the way you carry yourself. No one seeks advice from a fool, but everyone could learn something from a wise man." "Damn, your ass is like a black Confucius or something," Logan joked. "Confucius did say, when anger rises, think of the consequences," Marcus said with a sheepish grin. "Alright big bro, I'm gonna sit back and learn from you," responds Steele.

"Everyone thinks that this Walter Chase is the perp, so when we solve this case maybe the lieutenant and sergeant will get off my ass," says Steele. Marcus looks at Steele, "the first thing that you need to learn is to not fall into that trap that so many other detectives do. Before they have all the evidence, they've already made up their mind who's guilty. A good detective will gather the evidence and let that lead him to a suspect instead of pre-determining who the suspect is and trying to find evidence to support that theory. Take your time, do it by the numbers and eventually the smoke will fade. You'll see things a lot clearer then."

At zero eight hundred hours, Marcus' desk phone rings. He answers, "Detective Rose. Okay, someone will be right down to get her," he responds. "Hey Al, can you go to the front desk and get Ms. Flores and take her to interview room number one?" "Got it," responds Alverez. Marcus says to Steele," check out the interview from the observation room," then sits down to prepare himself mentally. As Marcus enters the interview room, he sees the housekeeper, Ms. Maria Flores sitting, clutching her purse with nervous anticipation. Ms. Flores is small framed, in her mid fifties with black hair. "Hola, como esta," Marcus greets her. "Muy bien gracias," she responds. "Mucho gusto," says Marcus as he reaches out and shakes her hand. Alvarez chuckles at Marcus' attempt to speak Spanish but she likes the fact that he tries. "My name is Detective Rose and you have already met Detective Alverez. We're hoping that you can give us some insight into the life of Laura Whittington." Ms. Flores shakes her head, okay. She spoke good English, but had a strong Latin accent.

Marcus: We talked briefly before at the house and I may ask you some of the same questions again. I just want to make sure that we get enough information to catch the person that did this. Do you actually live at Laura Whittington's house?

Ms. Flores: Yes, most of the time. I stay there Mondays through Friday and with my family on the weekends.

Marcus: Where were you before you arrived at Laura's home the morning she was found?

Ms. Flores: I spent the night at my daughter's house on Sunday night and I arrived at Laura's at four a.m., that Monday morning.

Marcus: Was the front door locked when you arrived and was the security alarm on?

Ms. Flores: Nods, yes.

Marcus: Did you notice anything out of order or peculiar when you entered the house?

Ms. Flores: No

Marcus: Did Laura have a boyfriend?

Ms. Flores: Yes, his name is Walter.

Marcus: What was their relationship like?

Ms. Flores: They used to argue and fight a lot.

Marcus: Really? What about?

Ms. Flores: Laura suspected that Walter was seeing other women and that made her jealous. He was a real jerk!

Marcus: Do you know if their fights ever became physical? Did he ever hit her?

Ms. Flores:  (she looked down and paused) Yes, I know that he slapped her a couple of times and once I saw him grab her by her shirt.

Marcus:  What did she do when he grabbed her?

Ms. Flores:  She fought back.  She grabbed his arms and attempted to break free but he was too strong.  He is a big man.  When he saw me, he let her go.

Marcus:  Did she ever call the police when they were fighting?

Ms. Flores:  No, I think that she was ashamed and didn't want anyone else to know.

Marcus:  Did Laura have any other male friends that came to the house?
Ms. Flores:  Yes, there was another man that she used to see.  I never knew his name though.

Marcus:  Used to see?  When did she stop seeing him and what did he look like?

Ms. Flores:  They stopped seeing each other about six months ago.  He was a white guy, tall, very handsome. He and Walter kinda looked alike and were about the same size.  I guess that was her type.

Marcus:  Tell me more about how he looked.  How old was he?  How long was his hair and did he have any facial hair?

Ms. Flores:  He looked to be in his late thirties.  He had short hair, kinda like a military person and he had a mustache.  He was kind of mysterious.  It was almost like she didn't want anybody to know about him.

Marcus:  Really!  Was she seeing this mystery man and Walter at the same time?

Ms. Flores:  I don't think so.  Once she started seeing Walter, I never saw the other man again.

Detective Alverez:  What makes you think that Laura didn't want anybody to know about him?

Ms. Flores:  She would always let him in through the back door, but Walter always used the front door and came in that way.  It's like she didn't want me to see him.

Detective Alverez:  If he came in through the back door, how did you actually see him?

Ms. Flores:  My room is at the back of the house.  I would see him enter the back yard from the alley and wait at the back door until Laura let him in.  He never

knocked and they were very quiet until they went upstairs.
Detective Alverez: What did you hear once they went upstairs?

Ms. Flores: Her bedroom is right over top of mine and I could hear them having sex through the vents in my room. Sometimes they were very loud.

Marcus: Do you know who killed Laura?

Ms. Flores: (She shook her head, no) I'm glad that you don't believe that she killed herself. Laura had every reason to live. She would never kill herself.

Marcus: Who do you think killed her?

Ms. Flores: I think Walter did it. He was very controlling and kind of evil, El Diablo.

Detective Alverez: Do you know why he would do something like that?

Ms. Flores: No, I don't. They argued a lot, maybe he just lost it.

Marcus: One last question. Besides you and her, did anyone else have keys to the house?

Ms Flores: Only her parents, but there was a spare set of keys that she kept in a kitchen drawer, but they're not there anymore.

Detective Alverez looked at Marcus and he nodded as if to say that was all the questions he had. "Thank you Ms. Flores, you have been very helpful. I'll walk you out," said Detective Alverez. She then led Ms. Flores out of the interview room and back downstairs. Detective Steele met Marcus in the squad room. "That was interesting. Ole Walter likes to beat women, can't wait to meet him," said Logan. "Yeah, I never understand why women stay," said Detective Alverez as she walked back into the squad room. "Furthermore, she had no children and plenty of daddy's money, why stay in an abusive relationship." "You tell us the answer to that Al, us men can't figure that kinda stuff out," said Logan.

"I'm just as puzzled as you guys. If that ever happened to me, he'd die of lead poison and I don't mean by stabbing him with a pencil," she joked. Logan looked at her and said "you know Al, I love an aggressive woman, we should do something aggressive together," as he smiled. Detective Alverez looked at Logan and asked, "is that the best you got Logan? Do other women really fall for those kind of lines?" "Pretty much, yeah," joked Logan. "You two need to get a room," laughed Marcus as he walked to the Lieutenant's office to talk about the interview.

"No kidding Al, I think that we should go out sometimes," said Logan. "As charming as that offer sounds, I don't have time for complications in my life Logan. I'm concentrating on the job and my family and most men don't want to be third in my life." Logan blatantly looked her up and down and said "I'll be third in your life...if you...let me." Detective Alverez interrupted, "is that all you men want? You're a cute guy Logan but I would never play where I work. It's messy and it's already hard enough for a woman to fit in here without you putting my business in the street." "I would never tell," said Logan. "You know, you and Ray both run those same tired lines. If you wanna have sex so bad, why don't you two get together," as she got up and walked away.

Logan watched her walk away (as usual). "Damn, she's phat as shit," he thought to himself. "One day I'll catch her in a moment of weakness and that will be all she wrote. I'll slow walk her, she's gotta give it to somebody sooner or later."

After a hard day, Detective Alverez liked to talk to her father. He was the main reason that she became a cop. He was her mentor and motivator. Only someone that had walked in her shoes could truly understand her trials and tribulations so she drove to her childhood home. She pulled into the driveway of her parent's home and parked. She sat back in her seat and reflected on her life in the police department and smiled. Getting her gold shield after only six years on the department was an accomplishment realized by only a few. She thought about the endless possibilities ahead of her and her future seemed bright.

But then a bolt of fear ran through her body and she hoped that one past mistake wouldn't ruin it all. Everybody has skeletons, she thought to herself. Even those higher ups aren't perfect. Surely some of them had made mistakes along the way too! Startled by her father's voice, "mija, why are you just sitting in the driveway, come inside," he said. "Just daydreaming papa," as she opened the car door and stepped outside. "Rough day," he asked as they hugged? "Nothing I can't handle," she responded. She wrapped her arm around his waist as they walked into the house.

"Sit, sit and tell me how everything is going. How's the life of a big time homicide detective," he asked. "Estoy bien, I'm good papa. Just working hard and trying to prove that I belong there." "Who are you trying to prove it to mija?" Before she could answer he began his usual discourse, "when I joined the police department forty two years ago, there weren't many Latinos on the force. Everyone made it hard on us because they really didn't want us there and they didn't think that we were smart enough to do the job. But we proved them wrong. How...with hard work and determination! Us along with our African American brothers stuck together and watched each other's backs because we were all we had. It took a while, but eventually the rest of the officers saw that we were no different from them."

"We were smart, we were strong and we were determined. Just like you are. When I look at you, I see it. I see your drive. I see your determination and I know that you will let nothing get in the way of you and success. Keep a strong mind and continue to look ahead and not behind. The only person that you need to prove it to is yourself. Once you have convinced yourself that you belong, everyone else will see it by the way you carry yourself. Don't get sidetracked and most of all don't let those men on the department distract you." "I know papa. I have my eye on the prize, but every once in a while I think about what we did seven years ago." "I don't want to discuss that" her father said. "Dredging the past up will accomplish nothing. What's done is done. End of discussion mija!" "Si papa, entiendo, I understand!

# Chapter Six
# Walter Chase

Marcus' desk phone rings "Detective Rose, can I help you? Right on time, okay someone will be down in a minute. Logan, can you go to the front desk and show Mr. Walter Chase and his lawyer to interview room number two?" Logan looks up from his desk, "you do know that I'm not a gopher, right?" Marcus gives Logan that look, the stink eye, as if to say, "take your ass down stairs and get the man." Marcus didn't use profanity, but he definitely had profane thoughts which most people could read just by looking at the expressions on his face. Without a word, Logan got up and went downstairs to retrieve Mr. Chase.

Marcus phoned Lieutenant O'Malley to let him know that he was about to interview the boyfriend. As Logan walked Mr. Chase through the squad room to the interview room, Detective Alverez stared at him as a cold chill ran down her spine. The expression on her face was as if she had seen a ghost. After Logan showed them to the interview room, he closed the door, removed his service weapon from its holster and put it in a lock box outside of the room. It was against police department regulations to interview potential suspects with their weapons on. If an interrogation turned physical, a suspect could potentially take one of their weapons and use it against them.  Marcus expressed the importance of always abiding by this rule.  Marcus then locked his weapon up.

As Logan was about to enter the interview room, Marcus stopped him, "no, we're gonna let them sit in there for a little while.  His lawyer set up the time for this interview, but we do things on our terms. We're in control, let' em sweat!"  After twenty minutes the detectives entered the room.  He noticed that Walter Chase was a large man.  Six feet three in height, good looking and looked to be in good shape.  He had a playboy look about him.  Dressed in slacks, button up white shirt with a v-neck sweater on top of it. Expensive leather loafers and black hair neatly trimmed and combed to the back.

On the surface he looked like a business man but just under the surface he looked like a man that didn't mind going out and getting his hands dirty.  He was neatly trimmed but rough around the edges. You should never judge a book by its cover, but first impressions can be telling.  They hadn't judged if he was a killer or not, but he had a look of danger.

Marcus:  Good morning gentlemen.  My name is Detective Rose and this is my partner, Detective Steele. Thanks for coming in.

Lawyer:  Detectives (he nods his head to them) I am Attorney Kenneth Marshall and I am representing Mr.

Chase. He has volunteered his services to assist you in this suicide investigation.

Marcus: What makes you think that this is a suicide investigation?

Attorney: Well, that's the information that we have.

Marcus: And where did you get your information from?

Attorney: That's not important detective. In any event, Mr. Chase is here to help.

Marcus: Great! Can I call you Walter (looking at Mr. Chase. Before Mr. Chase could answer) Walter, what was your relationship to Ms. Laura Whittington?

Mr. Chase: I guess you could say that she was my girlfriend.

Marcus: You guess...meaning that you're not sure?

Mr. Chase: Okay, we were dating (he said real smug like as he folded his arms).

Marcus: How long have you known Laura and how long have you been dating her?

Mr. Chase: I've know her for years but we have only been dating for about six months.

Marcus: When was the last time that you saw Laura?

Mr. Chase: I spent the night at her place on Saturday night and I left early Sunday morning.

Marcus: Exactly what time did you leave and was she alive when you left?

Mr. Chase: Of course she was, and I left around midnight.

Marcus: What was your relationship like? Were you guys in love?

Mr. Chase: (He breathed in deeply and covered his face with his hands) She was the love of my life.

Marcus: Did the two of you ever fight?

Mr. Chase: (He glanced over at his attorney before answering) We argued every once in a while.

Marcus: What kind of things did you argue about?

Mr. Chase: You know, normal girlfriend-boyfriend stuff.

Marcus: No, I don't know. I'm married and I'm not sure what normal girlfriend-boyfriend stuff is. He looks at Logan and asked, "do you?"

Logan: (Logan looks at Mr. Chase and asks) Can I call you Walt? (Before Mr. Chase could answer) Well Walt, I'm a single man and I'm not sure what normal girlfriend-boyfriend stuff is either. Could you be more specific?

Attorney: Detectives, Mr. Chase is here to assist you with your investigation and I'm not sure if what they argued about is germane to this investigation.

Logan: (Logan glanced over at the attorney with disgust and then turned his focus back to Mr. Chase) Have you ever had a physical fight with Laura? Have you ever slapped, hit, pushed or choked her?

Mr. Chase: Of course not. I would never hurt Laura, she meant the world to me.

(Marcus opened a folder that was on the desk and pulled out a picture of Laura as she laid on the kitchen floor, bloodied and dead. He reached across the table and handed the picture to Mr. Chase)

Marcus: Who do you think would do something like this to her?

Mr. Chase: (He stared at the picture and put his head down) I don't know who would hurt her (as he started sobbing). She had no enemies that I knew of, as his hands covered his face once more.

Marcus: Where were you on Monday morning? The morning that Laura was found.

Mr. Chase: I was at home...alone (as he continued to sob).

Marcus: (Marcus shuffled some papers around in the folder) Home...that would be 4524 Henry Lane in Bethesda?

Mr. Chase: Yes, that's where I live.

(Marcus looks over at Logan, as if to turn this part of the questioning over to him)

Logan: Look Walt, we all know that someone killed Laura and tried to make it seem like a suicide and if you look at any kind of cop shows, you know that the husband or the boyfriend is always the first person you wanna look at. Now, you are not a suspect, but we have to ask certain questions and do certain things to be able to rule you out.

Mr. Chase: (Nods his head with understanding)

Logan: We have reason to believe that Laura fought her attacker and may have scratched the killer. Will you take off your sweater and shirt so we can take a look at your upper body? Now, you can decline at which point we will get a court order to have a look see or in the spirit of cooperation, you can save us all the trouble of delaying the inevitable.

Mr. Chase looks over at his attorney and the attorney nods yes. He slowly stands up and removes his sweater then unbuttons his dress shirt. As he removes his shirt, there are visible scratches on both forearms and his chest.

Marcus: Looks like you've been in a fight Walter. How'd you get those scratches? Before you tell us another lie, understand that we know that you and Laura have had physical fights and that you at the least have slapped and grabbed her. It doesn't mean that you killed her but it does mean that you have not been forthcoming with us and it makes me wonder what else you have to hide.

Logan: If you really want to help yourself, now would be the time to start being totally truthful. Don't tell us what you think we wanna hear, tell us what happened. Before you answer, let me tell you a little story. I'm single just like you. I've got a feeling that you like the ladies and so do I. For guys like us, it's hard being faithful to just one lady. Doesn't make us bad guys and definitely doesn't make us murderers. It is what it is! We're gonna find out who did this and if you wanna get out the way of this train that's rolling down the tracks, now's the time to do so.

Mr. Chase: Okay, we used to fight a lot and sometimes it got physical. She always accused me of seeing other women and sometimes she would attack me. We were lying in bed last week and my cell phone rang. I didn't answer it and she asked me why I didn't answer it and what I was hiding. She tried to pick up my phone off the night stand and I got to it first. She lost it and started slapping and scratching me. These scratch marks on my arm and chest came from me trying to defend myself. She was the aggressor and I never laid a finger on her, at least not that night.

Logan: Can I see your phone Walt?

Mr. Chase unclips his phone from his waistband and hands it to Logan. Logan scrolls through it for a few minutes, makes a few notes and then hands it back to Mr. Chase.

Logan: Thanks, you have been very helpful. Now stand against the wall so that I can get a few pictures of your injuries. (Logan removes a digital camera from the file cabinet in the room and snaps several pictures). One last question, between midnight and four a.m., Monday morning, where were you?

Mr. Chase: I was at home.

Marcus: Thank you, Attorney Marshall and Mr. Chase. If we have any more questions, we'll contact you. You are free to leave now. Oh...one last thing. Do you have a key to Laura's house?

Mr. Chase: Yes...I have a spare key.

Marcus and Logan went to the squad room. Sergeant U, Lieutenant O'Malley and Detective Raymond Barlow had observed the interview from the observation room. They met Marcus and Logan in the squad room. Lieutenant O'Malley looked at Marcus and said, "Good interview. You too Detective Steele." Logan was surprised but pleased to hear that from the lieutenant.

"Did you notice anything strange about Mr. Chase," asked Marcus? "Yeah, all that crying and not one tear fell from his eyes," said Logan. "Why was he putting on that show? He's definitely hiding something," commented Marcus. "Also, Mr. Chase is left handed," remarked Logan. "When Marcus handed him the picture, he reached out and accepted it with his left hand. When I asked to see his phone, he handed it to me with his left hand. Definitely a strike against him. And he has a key to the house. He could have murdered her, left and locked the door behind him."

"Okay," chimed in Detective Barlow, "the rear neighbor saw a tall male in the alley behind the vic's house on the morning of the murder. I would say that Mr. Chase is tall. The vic scratched the killer and his DNA may be under her fingernails. Ole Walter has the scratches on his body consistent with that scenario. He's starting to look guilty to me." "But what's his motive. What does he have to gain from her death," asked Marcus?

"We have a few things to look into and then I suggest that we interview him again," said Logan. "What else do you think needs to be done," asked Lieutenant O'Malley? Logan responded, "When I asked to see his phone, I made note of his phone number. I'm gonna check his phone records and texts and see where that leads us. Also, gotta check and see if the phone was used the morning of the murder and where that puts him.

Talk to his neighbors to see if anyone can verify if he was really at home." "I'll go back to the scene and re-interview that rear neighbor. Maybe I can get a better description of the man that she saw in the alley," volunteered Ray. "Okay, thanks Ray," said Marcus. "Also, check and see if any of the neighbors have security cameras in the back of their houses that might have captured anyone in the alley."

"We also need to talk to her parents; they may be able to shed some light on her activities and who her friends were." We've only scratched the surface of this investigation. Slow and steady and we'll get our man," said Marcus. "Not too slow I hope. Closing this case will get the Chief off my back. She's riding my ass like a thoroughbred horse," joked Lieutenant O'Malley.

"Check with the alarm company and see if they've had any alarms from the house recently.

Good job detectives, I think we're on the right track," remarked the lieutenant. He looked Logan in the eye and nodded as if to indicate that he was pleased and walked to his office. Marcus and Logan looked at each other with amazement. "Damn, maybe he is human," remarked Logan. "Gotta hit 'em up for a new cruiser while he's in a good mood," joked Sergeant U. "I'm sure it won't last for long."

A.D. White

# Chapter Seven
# Logan, Man of Steele

Logan Armstrong Steele wasn't a complicated man. Born and raised in Brooklyn, New York by loving middle class, hard working parents. An only child who learned at an early age how to occupy his time so that he wouldn't be lonely. He kept busy by reading and playing every sport that was available to him. Baseball, football and basketball, but boxing was his true love. He was always big for his age, which didn't stop the neighborhood bullies from picking on him. He was quiet, a little awkward and they mistakenly took that for a weakness.

The older kids in the neighborhood watched Logan walking in and out of the neighborhood on way to his many sporting events, just minding his own business. Kids his age would make fun of him because they didn't understand him. Logan's parents didn't allow him to just hang out. He had to stay in the house unless he was doing something that they considered constructive and sports fit that bill. So the only time the neighborhood kids would see Logan is when he was walking to the local Boys Club to play whatever sport was in season. Because he didn't hang out with them, he became the target of their aggression.

Logan was twelve years old and on this particular day, he was walking to baseball practice. He had his glove in one hand and his baseball in the other. "Lurch," one of the kids called out to him. "Where you going?" "Baseball practice," he responded. "Let me see your baseball," he asked? Logan reluctantly tossed him the ball. "Thanks, it's mine now," he responded as the two other boys he was with laughed. Then the three of them walked away with the ball. These three boys were Logan's age but there were also boys that were fifteen and sixteen years old watching this exchange. The older boys didn't pick on Logan, but they didn't stop the three boys from picking on him either.

"Give me my ball back," demanded Logan. "Take it," was the ring leader's reply. Logan walked up to him and without saying a word smacked him in the face with his baseball glove in his left hand and punched him on the other side of his face with his right hand, knocking him to the ground. As he fell to the ground, he dropped the ball and it rolled a few feet away. "Oh snap," laughed the older boys as they were shocked at Logan's fearlessness. Logan looked at the other two boys and asked if they wanted the ball too. "Nah man, we don't want your ball," was their reply as they backed away. Logan picked up his ball and proceeded to baseball practice. That day Logan gained the respect of the neighborhood. That's all it took. Whip one person's ass and very few people will try to bully you after that. Logan became a neighborhood folk hero.

All kinds of stories grew out of that incident. The story changed a little every time it was told. It was said that Logan beat up all three boys. Another story was that Logan beat them all with a baseball bat, which earned him the nickname, "Slugger". The older boys were impressed with Logan and they befriended him. Now since Logan had the admiration of the older boys, the girls in the neighborhood all wanted to be his girlfriend. Such power at a young age!

His mystique only grew as he got older. At the recommendation of the older boys, Logan joined the boxing team and honed his fisticuff skills with formal training. Logan continued playing other sports and was best at basketball. He was awarded several basketball scholarships and eventually chose Howard University in Washington, D.C. Even though Logan was talented in basketball, he had no aspirations of playing professionally and much to the dismay of his parents chose a profession in law enforcement after graduating.

Logan joined the police department and graduated from the police academy at the top of his class. After the academy he was assigned to Eighth Police District and like most rookies was assigned to walk a foot beat after his initial training period. He was assigned to the Barry Farms Housing Projects, where the police were not welcomed. Regardless, he loved walking around the neighborhood in his uniform, playing the game of cat and mouse. The drug boys would stand on their corner but they would hide their stash somewhere nearby so that if they were searched by the police, nothing would be found on their person.

When someone drove up, one of them would go to the stash, get a bag of whatever they were selling and serve the customer. One of the other guys would hold all the money. A couple of guys were there as look outs. When they saw the police driving or walking up, they would give a signal and everyone would walk away. In the beginning, the drug boys would see him coming and they would just keep hanging out, which was seen as a sign of disrespect from the officer's view.

Logan had to make an example out of someone so he called for back-up. Raymond Barlow was in Logan's academy class. They both were assigned to the Eighth District and Ray had foot beat a few blocks over from Logan's beat. Ray walked over to assist Logan and a scout car also pulled up to help. The courts would call these gentlemen suspected drug dealers, but that wasn't reality. The police knew who the street level drug boys were, just like the drug boys knew who the police were. He couldn't allow them to just hang out there and ignore him.

Logan walked up to the four drug boys standing on the corner, "okay guys, put your hands on the fence," he yelled out to them as he approached. The four reluctantly turned around and placed their hands on the fence. "Why you fucking with us," one of men asked.

"Why you didn't walk your ass away when you saw me coming," Logan responded. "You not just gonna stand out here selling that shit on my beat. You gotta take that shit somewhere else or find another profession," Logan continued. Everyone here had been through this drill before and normally the police would search them and tell them that they had to leave. The drug boys would walk away and return later to continue their business or retrieve their drugs.

Today was different! Logan had gotten a call on his cell phone from one of the neighborhood residents and they told him where the drug boys were hiding their stash. Ray searched one guy and he had four hundred dollars in small bills in his pocket. "Oh, you're the accountant of the group," said Ray as he laughed. "Where'd you get this money from," Ray asked? "You can't have a job; your ass is out here night and day." "It's my mother's money. I'm going to the store for her," he responded. "Yeah, well tell yo mama that she can pick her money up at 8D, it belongs to the D.C. Government now," as Ray put the money in his pocket. "This some bullshit, you can't do that," the drug boy responded. "Yeah well, when you show me a pay stub, you can have it back," Ray responded "until then, its suspected proceeds of a crime."

Now Logan's source told him that the drugs were in an empty potato chip bag that was on the ground by a tree, appearing as if it was trash. Logan walked over by the tree and starting searching for the drugs. He saw the potato chip bag but didn't wanna go straight to it. If he did that, it would tell the drug boys that someone had snitched on them, so he went through the motions of searching all around before checking the potato chip bag. As he bent down to pick up the bag, he looked at the drug boys and saw the disgusted looks on their faces. Logan picked the bag up, looked inside and said, "Bingo. Lookie what we have here." He held the bag up in the air and asked, "does this belong to anyone?" All the drug boys just looked away. "I didn't think so," Logan responded.

The other officers asked the four drug boys for their names and ran it through with the dispatcher to make sure none of them had warrants. When the dispatcher responded with nothing found, Ray told them, "now ya'll can get the fuck outta here." They couldn't be arrested because the police didn't see them with the drugs and Logan's source wasn't willing to testify that they saw anyone in particular handle the drugs. This was common, but at least the drugs were confiscated which cut into their business. Logan got a ride to the police station and put the drugs into evidence, for destruction. After that day, whenever the drug boys saw Logan coming, they quickly walked away before he walked up to them.

Logan was tall, dark and handsome with a body that any man would be proud of. A deadly combination and just as fisticuffs came easy to Logan, attracting women came easier. Some of the women coined him, "Dark Gable" because he had the charm of Clark Gable and the charisma of Billy Dee Williams. Every source that he had in the neighborhood was a woman, all of whom were willing to please him.

He would sneak through the back doors when no one was looking. Some would have a meal waiting for him and others would be his meal. There was a motto among the foot beat officers. "A foot beat officer is never cold, wet or hungry." Which meant that a foot beat officer should be forging contacts in his area so that he had some place to go when it was cold outside, raining or if he needed a meal.

Logan perfected that theory and Ray was no different! Between the two of them, very few women were off limits. What was thought of by many as a strength, turned out to be their biggest weaknesses. Women were their kryptonite! When a woman was attractive and wanted them, neither knew how to say no. It didn't matter if they were someone's girl friend, fiancé or wife, they had their way with them. This always had the potential of making enemies for them and the last thing that you want is a jealous man out to get you. Every man knows that there are three things that you don't mess with. Another man's money, car or his woman! They both would eventually learn this the hard way.

After four years of walking a foot beat and making drug cases, Logan got assigned to the vice unit where he continued to shine. Most cops have their niche. Something that they did well. Some enforced traffic regulations, others tracked down drunk drivers. Logan excelled at making drug arrests. After a few years in vice, he was transferred to the departments, Narcotics Division, where he started off buying drugs as an undercover officer. During his time in Narcotics, he developed many sources throughout the city and was eventually recommended for the Homicide Division.

Logan and Marcus had become friends. Marcus saw qualities in Logan that reminded him of himself at a younger age. Who really knows why two people become friends, especially men. The two of them developed a bond. Marcus was older and more mature. He knew of Logan's reputation with the ladies and they had a long talk about respect.

If the two of them would become friends and Logan would be welcome at Marcus' home, he had to know the ground rules and Marcus had no problem laying them out. Marcus explained to him how his wife Gina was not only his best friend but his queen. His family meant everything to him and he was very careful of whom he allowed in his home. Home was his sanctuary. It was where he went for shelter and comfort and when he walked through his front door, he left all the evilness of the world outside. Marcus told him "I'm not a jealous man, per se, but don't ever disrespect my wife. What I would consider disrespect is looking at her in a sexual way or trying to be intimate with her. That would make you my enemy and I don't think that you want that."

"There are thousands of women outside of my home that are fair game and I don't really care what you do with them, but if you're gonna be welcome in my home, I have to trust you. Don't get me wrong, I trust my wife, but I also have to be able to trust you when we are on duty as well as off. My children are in my home and they have to be able to look up to any man that I call a friend. They learn by example and I am their protector and you also have to be their protector. If you see my children out in the street doing something wrong, you correct them and then tell me. I believe in the village concept. Family is everything!" Logan understood and appreciated Marcus' truthfulness. He looked up to Marcus and never disrespected him in any way.

The same day that they had interviewed Walter Chase, Logan went to Marcus' house that evening to discuss the case. He rang the doorbell and Marcus answered, "What's up Steele," as he stepped aside and Logan entered. "Uncle Logan," yelled M.J. and Brandon as they ran and jumped onto him, one on each side. As he always did, Logan made muscles with both arms. One boy grabbed his left arm and the other, the right arm as Logan lifted them in the air like a carnival ride and swung them around. The boys laughed with joy. "Okay, you two go to the play room. Logan and I have to talk." "Okay dad," as Logan put them down and they ran into the other room.

Logan and Marcus walked into his office down the hall from the front door. Gina walked in and gave him a hug, "hey Logan," then looked down at his shoes. "I'm taking them off now," said Logan as he bent down to untie his shoes. "I'm just about to put dinner on the table, you want something to eat," she asked? "When did you learn how to cook," he joked. Gina looked at him with a snarl, "don't play Logan. I'll put something in your food that you won't be able to digest." Logan looked at Marcus "you gonna let her do that to me," he joked? "Hey, you got yourself in this one all by yourself. I don't joke about my baby's cooking, I gotta live here." "Smart man," said Gina as she walked to the kitchen. "Yes, I would love a plate ma'am" as he laughs. "Hmm, hmm," Gina said as she closed the door behind her and continued to the kitchen.

"Alright, let's review the case. Let's go over what we do know and how that relates to Mr. Chase," says Marcus. "Okay," says Logan. "We know that the killer is left handed and that Walter Chase is also left handed. The killer must have locked the door behind him and Walter Chase has a key to the house. Walter Chase loosely fits the description of a man seen in the alley the morning of the crime. We know that the victim fought back and scratched the killer. Walter Chase has scratches on his forearms and chest area.

74

It's not looking good for Ole Walt, but I'm not totally convinced that he's our man. We have to figure out what he has to gain from her death. I think that she was his meal ticket, why would he kill her?" "Good point," remarked Marcus. "First thing in the morning, dump Walter's phone and see what we can glean from that. After that, check with the rear neighbor for a better description and if there are any cameras in the alley." "I thought Ray was gonna re-interview the neighbor," inquired Logan. "Ah...I want you to do it. I have something else for Ray to do."

"I'll have Alverez interview the mother. Ray can check with the alarm company and I'll follow up with the medical examiner for the tox screen. After all that's done, we'll re-interview Mr. Chase...got a few more questions I'd like to ask him." "Okay, sounds like a plan," remarked Logan. Gina knocks on the door. "Come in," answers Marcus. Gina opens the door and sticks her head in, "you two detectives ready to eat," she inquires?" "I'm starving Boo," answers Marcus. "Me too Boo," comments Logan. Gina shakes her head as she laughs, "keep playing Logan. Dinner's on the table."

# Chapter Eight
# I Call It Business

A couple of days had passed and all the detectives had gone out and gathered the information that Marcus requested. He felt that it was time to interview Walter Chase once more. Marcus loved the thrill of the chase and the second interview was always more enjoyable than the first. It was like a lion playing with its prey. The lion is in control and knows that he has his prey cornered. There's no where to run and no where to hide. Most importantly, unlike the first interview, he's armed with information that he didn't have the first time.

The second interview is like a test. He knows the answers to the questions he's about to ask and wants to see if his subject will lie or be truthful. Also, the first time they talked, Walter Chase was a witness, he is now a suspect. Lieutenant O'Malley, Sergeant U and Detective Barlow were in the room next door, which they coined, the observation deck, watching the interview through a mirrored glass. Once again, Walter Chase was accompanied by his attorney Kenneth Marshall.

Marcus: Attorney Marshall, Walter, thanks for coming in again.

Attorney: You're welcome Detective, what can we help you with?

Marcus: Things have changed since we first talked. The first thing that I want to do is advise you of your rights.

Walter: He jumped up from his chair, what...this is absurd. Am I a suspect? You've got to be kidding.

Marcus: No Walter, I wish that I was, but I'm not. I also have to let you know that this conversation is being recorded.

Attorney: Calm down Walter. Let's answer their questions and we can clear this whole thing up. (He looks at Marcus and Logan) We have nothing to hide.

Logan: Before we ask you any questions, you must understand what your rights are. You have the right to remain silent. You are not required to say anything to us at anytime or to answer any questions. Anything you say can be used against you in court. You have the right to talk to a lawyer for advice before we question you and to have him with you during questioning, a right that you are exercising now. If you cannot afford a lawyer, one will be provided for you. Do you understand these rights?

Walter: Yes

Logan: Do you wish to answer any questions?

Walter: Yes

Marcus: Where were you between the hours of twelve a.m., and five a.m., on the morning that Laura was found?

Walter: I was at home.

Marcus: We checked your cell phone records and discovered that at three thirty a.m., you made a call on your cell phone.

Walter: Okay, so!

Marcus: When anyone makes a call on their cell phone, signals are sent to the nearest cell phone towers and by finding out what cell towers the signals bounce off of, we can tell where the person was when he or she made that call. Guess where you were when you made that telephone call at three thirty in the morning?

Walter: (Silence!)

Marcus: You made the call from inside of Laura Whittington's home. You were at the scene of the crime. I also thought that it was strange that during the first interview, you never asked how Laura died. That's cause you already knew!

Walter: (Lowers his head)

Attorney: Okay gentlemen, this interview is over.

Logan: Attorney Marshall, it would be in your client's best interest to cooperate. Let me tell you why. Your client was at the scene of a murder. He had an intimate relationship with the victim and we know that they have gotten into physical altercations in the past. He has scratches on his arms and chest. The victim has skin from the killer under her fingernails and I'm pretty sure that the DNA will match your client. He has keys to the home and was able to enter and leave at will. We think that the killer is left handed and Walter just happens to be left handed also. This is all circumstantial, but it's starting to add up. We are prepared to arrest your client right now and he is not free to leave!

Walter: (looks at his attorney) I want to talk. I didn't kill Laura and I'm willing to tell them everything that I know.

Marcus: Great, we're all ears.

Walter: I went to Laura's about three thirty a.m., but when I got there, she was already dead. I found her in the kitchen. I saw the gun on the floor and the note on the counter. I didn't know that she had been murdered. I thought that she had committed suicide.

Marcus: Okay, so why didn't you call the police.

Walter: I was scared. I didn't want to be involved with a suicide.

Marcus: Are you kidding me? This was the love of your life. You're telling me that you were too scared to call the police, but you called some one else. Who did you call?

Walter: (Walter hunched his shoulders and sighed. Obviously struggling with the questions).

Logan: If we know where the phone call was made from, you know that we must know who you called. What we don't know is why you called Robert Whittington. What does he have to do with this?

There was silence as Walter contemplated the answer.

Logan: Take your time Walt, we've got all day. As a matter of fact, we're gonna leave the room and let you and your attorney talk this over. This just may be the most important decision of your life! (Marcus turns off the digital tape recorder, then he and Logan leave the room).

Walter and his attorney huddle together and talk. "I'm gonna tell them everything. I'm not going down for a murder I didn't commit," says Walter. "Okay, but you do know that Mr. Whittington is paying for my services and once he finds this out, you're gonna need another attorney...that is, unless you can afford my fee?" "Fuck you and your fee," Walter angrily says.

After ten minutes, Marcus and Logan return to the interview room.

Marcus: Well Walter, where did we leave off?

Walter: I called Robert Whittington because he's her father and I work for him.

Marcus: Doing what?

Walter: (His whole demeanor changed from the nice innocent guy to the cold calculating bastard that he really was). Let's just say that I collect and store information for him.

Marcus: I took the liberty of running your record and guess what I found? Don't answer...I found that you have a previous arrest for extortion. Does that have anything to do with your collection and storage job?

Attorney: Don't answer that!

Marcus: I retract that question counselor (says Marcus in a sarcastic tone). Okay, you called Robert Whittington and told him that you found his daughter dead. What did he say?

Walter: He told me not to touch anything, leave and lock the door behind me.

Marcus: Was the door locked when you arrived?

Walter: (he nodded his head) yes.

Marcus: I don't get it, why would he want you to leave and not notify the police.

Walter: Mr. Whittington said that he had interests to protect and that he didn't want his business connected to a suicide. He said that the maid would be there that morning and she would call the police once she discovered Laura.

Logan: So just like that, you leave. This is the woman that you say that you were so in love with. You just leave her?

Walter: I wasn't in love with her. I dated her for what she could do for me, what she could buy me. When we were together, I didn't have to spend any of my money. She was more than happy to pay for everything. The clothes that I wear and the car that I drive were all paid for by Laura. That's why I tolerated her!

Logan: Wow, a male gold digger.

Marcus: I think they call it a gigolo.

Walter: (He shrugged his shoulders) I call it business! And by the way, I was arrested for extortion but the charges were dropped.

Logan: Doesn't mean that you didn't do it!

Walter: Touché

Attorney: Okay Detectives, now that we've established that my client committed no crime, I think it's time for us to leave...unless you intend on arresting him.

Marcus: (He stood up and motioned towards the door) "Have a wonderful day, and oh...don't leave the area without letting us know".

Marcus, Logan, Detective Barlow, Sergeant U and Lieutenant O'Malley convened  in the squad room. "Wow, that was enlightening," said Lieutenant O'Malley. "This is getting messy; we need to interview the father ASAP." "Yeah, I gotta think about how to go at him. This could be tricky," said Marcus. "This guy is connected to the upper echelon of the city, gotta brief the Chief on this one," says Lieutenant O'Malley as he heads towards the door. "Alverez is interviewing the mother as we speak. I wonder how much she knows. How deep does this run," commented Logan as he looks at Marcus. "Don't know yet, but time will tell!"

# Chapter Nine
# Laura Whittington

As Detective Alverez sat with Laura's mom, she talked about Laura's life. Her motherly pride and tearful recollection of her daughter's life painted a picture of a mother's love and a father's disappointment. Laura was a beautiful person with a kind heart. She saw the best in everybody, even when they were at their worst. She had the gift of gab and would talk to anyone that she came in contact with. She didn't care if you were a model citizen or a bum on the street. She saw a redeeming quality in everyone, which explained the poor choices in the men she dated.

Laura was expected to go to college and she did. Graduating at the top of her class but that wasn't good enough for Robert Whittington. He expected her to be the Valedictorian and she wasn't. She majored in business just to impress him, but even that didn't work.

She was beautiful, smart and kind but nothing that she did seemed to please her father and she couldn't figure out why. She looked up to him and spent her whole life trying to please him. She had an eye for fashion and really wanted to design clothes, but knew that her father would not approve of that for a major.

She thought that she had to be good in business just to get his attention.

Laura had a since of responsibility. She knew that she was privileged and wanted to give something back. She volunteered at a homeless shelter in D.C. That is until her father found out and forbid her to continue. Laura then volunteered her time reading to the elderly at a nursing home in Georgetown.

She wasn't allowed to date until she was eighteen because Robert Whittington did not want outside influences distracting Laura from the path that he chose for her.

Maureen Whittington saw her daughter in a very different light. There was nothing that Laura could do to disappoint her. She took pride in all her daughter's achievements. From placing third place in her high school swim meet to learning how to play the violin. They talked on the phone everyday. They had to hear each others voice to start or complete their day. She was the light in her mother's eyes and the breath in her life and now she was gone. Maureen now started to resent Robert for not seeing their daughter as she did. Laura never knew why she wasn't good enough for her father, but Maureen did!

# Chapter Ten
## Does Your Dog Bite?

Two days had passed since Walter Chase's interrogation. The squad had been gathering more and more evidence in the pursuit of justice. Marcus had a ritual, whenever he interviewed a suspect or a witness that could become a suspect. He wanted to know everything possible about that person. Their financial status, their business dealings and their personal life were all points of interest. It was like going into battle. If a boxer had a big fight coming up, he would train for the fight. If an executive had an important meeting, he or she would study for the meeting so that he were prepared.

This was no different for Marcus. He prepared himself by gathering every bit of information about Robert Whittington as he could legally obtain. He was a very powerful man. Most of the time, their high powered lawyers wouldn't allow them to be interviewed, at most they would send you a sworn statement. But for some unknown reason, Mr. Whittington agreed to be interviewed. Marcus knew that he would only get one chance to interview him and wanted to make the best of it.

This wasn't a cat and mouse game, or even the lion and his prey.  This was going to be Lion vs. Lion and only the strong would survive.  Detective Alverez had been very helpful.  She interviewed his wife two days ago and armed Marcus with valuable information.

The morning of the interview, the squad met to discuss the merits of the case.  Marcus addresses the squad.  "The Medical Examiner was able to get DNA from underneath the victim's fingernails even though there was an attempt to remove the evidence by the killer.  The FBI has a DNA database and we have to send our sample to them but it usually takes a few months to get back any results."  Detective Barlow interrupted, "I've got a contact over there and I can get the results a little faster."  "Let me guess…it's a woman," said Big Russ.  "Hey, don't hate the player, hate the game," Detective Barlow joked.  "Okay, take care of it," said Marcus.

Marcus continued, "the toxicology report came back and the victim had Ambien in her system.  Al found out from the mother that the victim was suffering from insomnia which explains why that drug would be in her system.  The gun found on the scene was registered to the victim and ballistics show that it was the weapon that she was shot with."  From everything that we know, the killer must have known the victim," said Big Russ.  "It's definitely not random and nothing was missing, so it's not a burglary gone wrong," said Detective Alverez.

"The boyfriend says that he found the victim prior to the housekeeper arriving. He works for the victim's father and called him from inside the residence. The father tells the boyfriend to leave and lock the door behind him. Some crap about not wanting her death to affect his business dealings." "Wow, what kind of cold bastard is he," commented Detective Alverez. "We're gonna find that out later today," injected Logan. "Al, what other information did you get from interviewing the mother," asked Marcus? Detective Alverez stood up and addressed the squad.

"The mother's name is Maureen Whittington. She is fifty two years old and was visibly disturbed by her daughter's death. Says that they were very close and they talked everyday. She knew that her daughter was seeing Walter Chase but did not mention that Mr. Chase worked for her husband. Not sure if she knew that. Apparently, her husband was very secretive about his business and did not tell her much about what he did daily. He made the money and she spent it."

"She knew that Laura and Mr. Chase fought because Laura thought he was seeing other women, but the mother did not think that Mr. Chase was capable of killing her. She told me about another man that Laura used to see. Laura never told her his name or what profession this guy was in, but she knew he was "common," as she put it. Because this guy was a regular dude and not of money, the mother encouraged her to stop seeing him. She knew that Mr. Whittington would not approve of anyone that wasn't of their class."

"That eliminates all of us," Sergeant U joked. "Apparently, this guy didn't take the break up well, went ballistic. She gave me Laura's best friends name and phone number. Gonna see if she can tell me who this guy is. As far as the mother knows, Laura had no enemies and had no idea who would want to harm her daughter. That's all I got." "Thanks Al, let me know when you reach the best friend," said Marcus. Detective Alverez nods her head in agreement.

"Ray," said Marcus, "what did you find out on your re-canvass?" Ray stood up and said "I re-interviewed the neighbor who lives directly behind the victim's house and she couldn't tell me anything further than she saw a tall male walking in the alley, wearing dark clothes at about zero three hundred hours, the morning of the homicide. Couldn't tell if he was black, white or Hispanic. None of the other neighbors had cameras that captured the rear of Laura Whittington's house or the alley adjacent to her house. Pretty much a dead end."

"Thanks Ray," said Marcus. "What time is Mr. Whittington set to come in," asked Lieutenant O'Malley"? "Thirteen hundred hours sir," replied Marcus. "Logan and I will be getting our game plan together until then." "Sarge and I will be in the observation deck during the interview. Good luck men," said Lieutenant O'Malley.

Marcus and Logan went to their desks to outline their strategy. "Marcus, I'm pretty much ready. I know what questions I want to ask him," says Logan. "There is no substitute for preparation young detective. You know what questions you want to ask him but do you know in what order you want to ask them," asked Marcus? Logan looked confused "what do you mean?"

Marcus laughs and shakes his head "let me give you an example: A man walks up to a boy and a dog and asks does your dog bite? The boy responds, no. The man reaches to pet the dog and the dog bites the crap out of him. The man says to the boy, I thought you said that your dog doesn't bite. The boy responds, that's not my dog. Instead of asking first, does your dog bite, he should have asked is this your dog." The light turned on in Logan's head as he began to understand that he had much more to learn, but he knew that he was where he was supposed to be and learning from the right person.

At thirteen hundred hours, Robert Whittington and his high powered lawyer were right on time. They were brought to the interview room by Detective Barlow. As usual, Marcus made them wait about fifteen minutes before he and Logan entered the room. Mr. Whittington was sixty years old, six feet tall with a medium build. He was dressed in a very expensive looking navy blue suit with brown shoes. Grey hair that was neatly trimmed and clean shaven about the face.

He had an air of invincibility about him and cold dark eyes that would bring a chill to most.

His attorney was a few inches shorter and much younger with a shaven head and salt and pepper beard. He wore a tailor made black suit, white shirt with a red silk tie and handkerchief to match. A graduate of Howard University's Law School who had a reputation of defending the lawless. Mr. Whittington had brought out the big guns from the very start which signaled to Marcus that he had something to hide.

Marcus: Hello gentlemen, my name is Detective Rose and this is my partner Detective Steele (as he pointed to Logan).

Attorney: My name is Daryl White and I am counsel for Mr. Whittington. Mr. Whittington has taken time out of his busy schedule to come here today and we would have appreciated it, if the process would have started at the scheduled time.

Marcus: As I am appreciative of Mr. Whittington's time, fifteen minutes should not dampen his desire to help us solve the murder of his daughter. I have to let you know that this interview will be recorded (as Logan flipped the switch on the wall that started the recording).

Attorney: (Lifted his briefcase from the floor and placed it on the interview table. He flicked open the latches of the briefcase and opened it, taking out a small digital recorder) You don't mind if we record this session as well (as he pressed play on his recorder)?

Marcus:  Not at all.

Logan:  (thought to himself "this asshole is recording us, recording him, damn!")

Attorney:  Is my client a suspect or a witness?

Marcus:  Your client is a witness at this time.  In the event that he becomes a suspect, you will be the first to know.

Robert Whittington:  (Stares intently at Marcus as if to intimidate him)

Marcus:  Mr. Whittington, could you tell me your whole name and what you do for living?

Mr. Whittington:  Robert Nathaniel Whittington and I am the president, CEO and owner of Whittington Pharmaceuticals.

Marcus:  Do you own land on Georgia Avenue, northwest in Washington, D.C.?

Mr. Whittington:  Yes (wondering how he knew that and what it has to do with his daughter's murder).

Marcus: Do you also own land in Tyson's Corner, Virginia?

Mr. Whittington: Yes. Apparently you've done your homework, but what does this have to do with this case?

Marcus: This case? You mean the murder of your daughter?

Mr. Whittington: (he just stared at Marcus without answering)

Marcus: Apparently you make a living from more than just your pharmaceutical company?

Mr. Whittington: Of course, it's the American way! I'm an opportunist; I make money in various ways.

Marcus: Is that what drives you. Money, that is?

Mr. Whittington: (he continued staring at Marcus without answering that question)

Marcus: Do you know Mr. Walter Chase?

Mr. Whittington: Yes (continues staring at Marcus)

Marcus: (sensing that his attorney has told him to only give short to the point answers) How do you know Mr. Chase?

Mr. Whittington:  He dated my daughter Laura.

Marcus:  Do you employ Mr. Chase?

Mr. Whittington:  Yes

Marcus:  Doing what?

Mr. Whittington:  He gathers information for me.

Marcus:  Could you be more specific?

Mr. Whittington:  No!

Marcus:  Are you aware that Mr. Chase entered your daughter's house the morning that she was murdered and found her dead?

Mr. Whittington:  I am.

Marcus:  Did he call you from Laura's house?

Mr. Whittington:  He did.

Marcus:  Why would he call you instead of the police and what did you tell him?

Mr. Whittington:  As to why he called me first, you would have to ask him that.  What did I tell him?  I told him not to touch anything, leave the house and lock the door behind him.

Marcus: You see, that's puzzling to me. Why would you tell him to do that? He just told you that your daughter was dead and you tell him to leave? Why?

Mr. Whittington: Mr. Chase works for me and I did not want her death to affect my business dealings in anyway.

Marcus: That money thing again, huh?

Attorney: If I may? Mr. Chase advised Mr. Whittington that Laura Whittington had shot herself and was deceased. Not knowing that a crime had been committed, he advised Mr. Chase to leave knowing full well that the maid would be arriving shortly and would call the authorities. In doing so, there was no crime committed by Mr. Whittington or Mr. Chase.

Marcus: (leaned back in his chair while stroking the hairs on his goatee) What can you tell me about your daughter's murder?

Mr. Whittington: Nothing.

Marcus: You have a lot of business dealing in D.C., Maryland and Virginia. You acquire land under...let's say under questionable tactics and sell that land for much higher profit. In doing so, you must have made a few enemies. Does anyone come to mind that might have done this (sliding a picture of Laura's dead body across the table) to him?

Mr. Whittington: (looked down at the picture, then back at Marcus, saying with no emotion) No .

Marcus: You know Mr. Whittington, there's a process that most people go through when dealing with the death of a loved one. The loved one experiences denial, anger, bargaining, depression and lastly, acceptance.

Attorney: We're familiar with the Kubler-Ross Model Detective.

Marcus: You've seemed to gone straight to acceptance with no emotional effects of your daughter's death at all. Even the picture of her dead body didn't phase you. You may not have killed her, but what you did was cold and calculating. Laura's not your biological daughter, is she?

Mr. Whittington: No...she's not. Her mother was pregnant with Laura when we met and I raised her as my own.

Marcus: Do you even care that she's gone or who killed her?

Mr. Whittington: Of course I do (he said in a lackadaisical manner)

Marcus: Did you kill her or do you know who killed her?

Mr. Whittington: Absolutely not!

Marcus: Mr. Whittington, I'm curious. How would Mr. Chase finding your daughter's body have an effect on your business? Pharmaceuticals and death go hand in hand! (he said in a sarcastic tone)

Attorney: Okay (he interrupted) unless you plan to arrest my client, this interview is over!

Marcus: (looking into his cold dark eyes) Mr. Whittington, I haven't totally figured you out yet but in time I will. There's a lot more to you that meets the eye. I want you to know that I'm watching. I'll know when you acquire property. I'll know if you're involved in a traffic accident. I'll know if any of your many vehicles receive a traffic tickets. I'll even know when you wash your hands and when you slip up, I'll know that too. (Marcus stood up and looked at Mr. Whittington's attorney) Your client's free to go.

Mr. Whittington: Don't make promises that you can't keep, Detective.

Logan shows Mr. Whittington and his attorney the way out and then returns to the squad room. "Wow, that was (searching for an adjective to describe what he had just witnessed) interesting!" "To say the least," added

Lieutenant O'Malley. "I think you just made an enemy Marcus," says Detective Barlow. "I just want him looking over his shoulder," Marcus explained. "I want him to think of me as the boogey man. Never knowing when I'm gonna jump out and ruin his day. I don't think that he had anything to do with the death of Laura Whittington, but he's doing something illegal and when I find out what, I'll make him pay!"

"How did you know that Laura Whittington was not his biological child" asked Logan? "Al interviewed the mother the other day and she said that nothing that Laura did was ever good enough for him. After a little digging, she described her husband as controlling, manipulative and evil and he only verified that here today. There is no way that a father could take the death of his daughter so matter of fact. Even when he saw the picture of her dead body, he showed no emotion. That told me that he couldn't have been her biological father."

"That was good work in there today, Marcus, but we're no closer to finding the person who murdered Ms. Whittington," said Sergeant U. "I've got a few more ideas," said Marcus as he walked to his desk. "Gotta brief the Chief on the interview, we'll talk later Marcus," said Lieutenant O'Malley as he walked out, followed by Sergeant U. "Anything else you need me to do Marcus," asked Detective Barlow? "Yeah, find out from Al if she's contacted the victim's best friend yet. I'm sure she'll lead us to that other guy." "Okay, got it," said Detective Barlow as he leaves the squad room.

As Marcus and Logan sit at their desks, "how did you get all the info on his land purchases and will you really know when he washes his hands," Logan half heartedly joked? We have a computer system called C.L.E.A.R. I'll have Al train you on it. This system pulls real time information from multiple databases. Anything he does and I mean anything he does that uses his social security number will be listed the moment he does it. He's dirty as hell so I don't think he actually washes his hands," joked Marcus.

Marcus gave Logan a real serious look, "I got a couple of things I need you to check on." As Detective Alverez walks into the squad room, Marcus says "Al, I need your help with something." "Anything for you Marcus," she responded. Logan gave her a look of disgust this time and mumbled, "anything for you Marcus." Marcus laughed and said "Steele, get it together. Train Logan on C.L.E.A.R., while you look into any business dealings of Mr. Robert Whittington." "Got it. Come on Logan," as she walked away and motioned for Logan to follow. As usual, Logan stared at her ass as he followed. Al whistled and said "here boy," as Logan followed. "Real funny Al. You calling me a dog" Logan asked? "If the shoe fits," was her response.

# Chapter Eleven
## Detective Raymond Barlow

Detective Raymond Barlow grew up in Newark, New Jersey. He graduated from Montclair State University in New Jersey and then decided to go to the big city, Washington D.C. Long before then, Ray and his older sister were raised by their mother and father in a middle class setting. Ray was always outgoing and popular with the ladies. Some of his black friends jokingly called him L.L. Cool Ray (ladies love cool Ray) after one of his favorite rappers L.L. Cool J.

Ray weaved his way through both communities, white and black and was accepted by both. He was like a chameleon. He could adapt to whatever community and situation he was in and with whatever friends he was with. Ray had what was called a ghetto pass, meaning that when he was with his black friends he was one of them and could use the N-Word without retribution. When with his white friends, he used it also. But to really understand Raymond Barlow, we have to look inside of his home.

His father was an abusive alcoholic who regularly beat his mother. Ray grew up hearing and seeing the fighting inside of his home all of his life. It was normal for him to come home and see his mother with bruises inflicted by his father. It was normal to hear his father yelling at the top of his lungs. His father was dominant and his mother was submissive which didn't stop the ass whippings. Ray and his sister feared their father. They rarely got beaten because they always submitted to their father's demands. It was the law of the land.

When a boy grows up in an abusive environment he can go in one of two directions. He could be the kind of person that despises violence and never wants to treat a woman the way his mother was treated, or, he could grow up to be just like his daddy. Ray grew up to be an evolved model of his father. Ray didn't normally beat women. He didn't have to. He ruled by intimidation.

He was aggressive and intimidated them to get their compliance in a relationship. When his high school sweetheart wanted to go out with her girlfriends, Ray would look at her and tell her that she wasn't going out. With his size and attitude, most would do as he commanded. Ray was six feet tall in middle school, eventually growing only three more inches until he reached adulthood. He saw violence inside and outside of his home, so fighting wasn't a problem for him. Ray grew up to be a bully of men and women. He didn't discriminate. He had an only the strong survive mentality. If you were weak, you were his prey.

Ray was a fitness buff. A towering figure to most. Good looking and with this outgoing personality, women flocked to him, at least until they got to really know him. He was used to getting what he wanted. He was a star high school basketball player and went to college on a basketball scholarship. He wasn't NBA material, but he was pretty good. His favorite thing to do was driving to the baseline and pushing people around. He thrived off the contact of bodies slamming into each other which satisfied his propensity for violence.

Whenever he played a hard game of basketball, he was getting his fix of aggression. When he got really pissed off about something, he would play basketball or go to the gym as an outlet. Over the years he learned how to contain his violent tendencies but just like any dysfunction, it couldn't be hidden all the time. Eventually it would rear its ugly head at the wrong time.

Ray joined the police department and after the academy was assigned to the Eighth Police District. He and Logan became friends and used to hang out after work with the same group of officers. Drinking and chasing women! They were hell raisers. They had guns, badges and when mixed with alcohol, let's just say it wasn't a great combination. They were on the top of the world. Working hard and having fun at night.

The only cure for the disease they had was maturity. Some of the group eventually matured and went on to have good careers and others eventually did something reckless and lost their jobs. The attrition rate was astonishing. The police department didn't put up with lawlessness in their ranks and if exposed, you were expendable. Ray eventually passed the test to become an investigator and after a year of investigating minor crimes was promoted to Detective Second Grade. After years of good detective work, he got a break and was transferred to the Homicide Division where he was re-united with his old friend Logan Steele.

Ray was still a single man. Still hanging out at bars at night and by now he was drinking to numb the pain of being a homicide detective. These detectives saw death on a regular basis. Seeing dead bodies were their norm. Just as normal as a secretary typing a memo. Just as normal as an executive going to a staff meeting and just as normal as a mechanic changing the brakes on your car. Some detectives developed a morbid sense of humor. Some drank alcohol in excess and some acted out in anger. All of this was done unconsciously as a coping mechanism to deal with the trauma that was inflicted upon them, voluntarily and on a regular basis.

Seeing a dead child that had been beaten by the baby sitter, the man lying in the street riddled with gun shots, looking up at you as he takes his last breath and the elderly woman that was beaten to death when she interrupted a burglar. All this took a toll on the detectives and using unhealthy coping mechanisms hid the pain and pushed it to the rear of their unconsciousness. Tucked neatly away until it's eventual re-emergence. That is unless they found healthy ways to deal with the trauma of their profession. Ray had come from a dysfunctional background so finding unhealthy ways to deal with the job was just par for the course.

Ray loved the bar scene in Georgetown where the ratio was six women to every man. For a player like Ray, it was nearly impossible for him not to find a woman looking for a good time. His good looks were the icebreaker and once he was able to determine what they were looking for in a man, he became that man. He would become whatever they were seeking. If he needed to be understanding, he would be that. If he needed to be intelligent to get next to them, he could be that too. If he needed to be that bad boy, he could definitely take on that role. He did and said whatever it took to accomplish his goal and his goal was to have meaningless sex. At least it was meaningless to him.

That is until he met her! She was young and pretty with a beautiful smile. Bright and full of life. He met her and for the first time, he thought about the future with a woman. Through the maze, he saw her across a crowded bar and he walked up to her, "can I take your order," Ray asked? She looked at him with amazement, "I'm sorry, I didn't realize that you worked here. Yes, I'll have a Apple Martini." "Coming right up", he responded as he walked away.

Ray came back a few minutes later with her drink and placed it in front of her. "How much do I owe you," she asked? "Just a few minutes of your time," he said, as he sat down next to her. She laughed, "you don't work here, do you," she asked? "No I don't," as he smiled, "I just had to meet you." I'm not sure what it is about some people that gives them the ability to capture your heart when others don't have a chance, but she was that person for Ray. The one that could turn his life around and change his views on dating.

They talked for a few hours and exchanged numbers. They started dating and fell for one another hard and fast. Ray told only a few of his buddies about her; he hoped that this wasn't too good to be true. They dated a few months and in his mind, all was well. At least it was until she told him that she no longer wanted to see him. Ray wanted to know why, but she couldn't explain it to his satisfaction. She said that she wanted to see other people and it was best if he did too. She ripped his heart out. The one person that was able to get close to him, broke his heart. Karma is a bitch! What you do to others will eventually come full circle and bite you right in the ass.

Ray never cared about the hearts that he was breaking, now his heart was the one being broken. No matter who you are, there's someone out there that can disarm you. She told him something that he had told many others. "It was not my intention to hurt you." Wow, what irony. She did exactly what she hadn't intended and what he had done to many others. Ray wished that he had never met her; his life was sent into a tail spin.  Ray was drinking heavier and womanizing twice as much as he did before.  Ray was on a course for self destruction and it wasn't pretty.

# Chapter Twelve
# A Deal With the Devil

In 2006 Officer Bennie Alverez was an experienced street officer with thirty six years under his belt. He joined the department in a time when minorities weren't treated equally and their chances for advancement didn't come easy. But he enjoyed his job and worked hard to do things the right way. He was a proud man and wanted nothing more but to set a good example for his children. Bennie always wanted a son to follow in his footsteps but after siring four girls he gave up on that dream.

His oldest daughter, Katelyn strived to be that son that he never had. She was the tomboy of the group. She played sports and ran around with the boys in the neighborhood and was just as tough as any of them. Who knew that she would grow up to be pretty and sexy on the outside, but still rough and tough on the inside? She watched baseball with her father and even drank beers with him once she became of age. It came as no surprise to anyone when she applied to be a police officer.

Katelyn joined the department the year of Bennie's retirement. As hard as Bennie tried to be that example, he had one crutch. No, make that two.

Gambling and drinking. Over the years, Bennie played poker in as many backdoor poker games that he could find. Sometimes he would win but most of the time he would leave drunk, broke and dejected. Bennie's wife knew all about it, but she accepted him as he was. Those two crutches aside, Bennie was a good husband and a great father to his children. They struggled financially at times but Bennie always came up with a way to pay the bills. There was always food on the table for his girls.

After thirty six years on the department, he hoped that he had a little more to show for his hard work. One night, Katelyn received a radio run for a burglar alarm at a real estate business in Georgetown. Bennie happened to be working that night also, and as he often did, he went to assist his baby girl. When Katelyn arrived at the business, the front door was locked but she could hear the alarm sounding. She walked around to the back and noticed that the back door was ajar.

She radioed the dispatcher what she had found as Bennie arrived on scene. Since they were not sure if anyone was still inside, they radioed for a K-9 unit to search the premises, which they did and found no one inside. The K-9 officer then left the scene. Katelyn and Bennie walked around the business to see if there were obvious signs of anything taken or destroyed.

During their search, Bennie opened a closet door that had a safe inside. He turned the handle and much to his amazement, the safe opened.  Shocked, Bennie looked inside and discovered that the safe was full of money.  Bennie was scheduled to retire in two months and saw his chance to pay off some much needed bills before then.  He stood there for a moment just staring at the money.  Then he grabbed two stacks of bills and stuffed them in the inside pocket of his police jacket just as Katelyn was entering the room.

Katelyn stood their in amazement as Bennie looked into her eyes as if to plead for her silence. Katelyn walked out of the room as if she saw nothing. Bennie closed and lock the safe and a few minutes later, the custodian for the business arrived.  The custodian checked the place and did not notice that anything had been taken.  He locked the place up and Katelyn took an attempted burglary report, noting that nothing was missing.

Months passed and they never spoke of that night until they were contacted by a man named Walter at the police station.  Walter explained to Bennie and Katelyn that he worked for the owner of the real estate business and that the owner wanted to meet with them to thank them for protecting his business.  It felt like a set up to both of them, but they saw no other way but to attend the meeting.

As they arrived, Walter showed them to the office in the back.  The same office that contained the safe.

The owner identified himself as Robert and asked them to be seated. Walter sat in a chair in the dark corner of the room observing the meeting. There the two police officers sat in anticipation wondering what this was really about. They hoped that it wasn't about the money but that would have been too good to be true.

As they sat, the owner said, "I obtained a copy of the police report and saw that the two of you responded to my business a few months ago when the reported burglars broke in. I'd like to thank you for your service." They both nodded. "By the way, I noticed that you have the same last name, are you two related?" "Yes," answered Bennie. "This is my daughter." "You must be very proud," responded Robert. Bennie nodded once more. "Well, I never like to beat around the bush, so I'm going to get straight to the point.

In addition to the alarm, I have video surveillance of the premises and there's something that I want you to see." Robert picked up a remote control on his desk and pointed it at the flat screen television on the wall, turning it on. He then used another remote control to start the video. The video that clearly showed Bennie opening the safe, removing two stacks of money and placing it into his pockets. "The clarity is remarkable, wouldn't you agree," asked Robert? Bennie sighed, "yeah, it's pretty good." The video also captured Katelyn standing there watching Bennie, then Robert cut if off.

Robert leaned back in his chair "officers, we have a problem. Twenty thousand dollars was missing from my safe and the police report doesn't mention it. I'm a business man, mind you. What do you think that I should do about this?" Bennie leaned forward, "listen, I know what I did was wrong. I still have most of the money and I can give it back to you." "It's not about the money," Robert responded. "It's about trust. We trust the officers in this city to do the right thing and I'm sure that most of them do. But not everyone."

Bennie and Katelyn sat there in silence. "Police officers have a pretty hard time in jail and I would hate for that to happen to the two of you, but I have a solution." "Let my daughter leave, she has nothing to do with this. We can discuss how I can pay you back," said Bennie. "I beg to differ," Robert responded. "She saw what you did and that makes her part of it. You involved your daughter, but I have a solution."

They both looked at Robert with baited breath. "Keep the money. Obviously you needed it or you wouldn't have taken it. Police officers don't get paid a lot of money. Think of it as a contribution" he said. "A contribution to what," Bennie asked. "A contribution for your cooperation," Robert responded. "What do I have to do" Bennie inquired? "Not I, we. You're not in this by yourself," responded Robert. As much as you would like for this not to involve your daughter, it does. But you don't have to do anything for it...right now! There may come a time when I need a favor and the two of you have been paid in advance for that favor. It's up to you. You can agree to be my friends or Internal Affairs can view the tape. Your choice, but you don't have a lot of time to decide. I'm gonna need to know right now how you want me to handle this."

"You want nothing right now," Bennie asked? "That's correct; you can walk out of here with a clean conscious. The money's yours. I may or may not need something from you in the future," said Robert. Bennie and Katelyn looked into Robert's cold, dark eyes and agreed to his terms. They had just made a deal with the devil! Bennie retired from the police department two months later.

# Chapter Thirteen
## Pay Day

Detective Alverez started training Logan on the C.L.E.A.R., computer system. He learned as she looked into Robert Whittington's public records. You name it; his financial records, bank accounts, tax records, driving record, everything that could be found.

After a full day of delving into his life, she found something. She wasn't an accountant but it appeared that income obtained from land that Robert Whittington acquired and sold hadn't been reported to the IRS and subsequently, taxes weren't paid on that income. She contacted the department's Financial Crimes and Fraud Unit. They were the experts on white collar crime.

She gave them what she had found and they took over the investigation into his finances. They also discovered something else. Mr. Whittington had several different businesses with different business names. These businesses were listed as being co-owned by various people, omitting Mr. Whittington as the other co-owner. But if you dug deep enough into the dummy corporations, Mr. Robert Whittington's name emerged. One particular business was called South of the River Loan Company and the listed co-owner was Walter Chase.

This rang a bell for Logan. He remembered that about two years ago, this business burned down and a dead body was found inside. The body was so badly burned that identifying it was impossible and the cause of death could not be determined. Basically, they didn't know if the fire killed the person or if the person was already deceased before the fire was set. It was an unsolved case. Al and Logan knew that digging into this case would make Robert Whittington and Walter Chase very uncomfortable.

Detective Alverez had a much bigger problem though! When Walter Chase came in for his interview as the boyfriend of Laura Whittington, she recognized him from her past. He was the same Walter that worked for the owner of the real estate business that her father had taken the money from. The owner, "Robert" was none other than Robert Whittington. She knew that if she made them too uncomfortable that they could ruin not only her career, but her life also. Logan could tell that something was wrong with Al, but he had no idea of the magnitude. Al had to do something that she wasn't looking forward to; talk to her father about a subject that he had been avoiding for years.

As she drove to her father's house she played in her head all the possible scenarios that she could imagine. She was driving slowly, not in any hurry to have this conversation. She pulled into the driveway and sat in her car. Once again, her father came out of the house and approached her car, "mija, why are just sitting out in the driveway? Come inside." As he looked at the expression on her face he asked, "what's wrong baby girl?" "I've seen Walter," she replied. "Walter who," was his next question? She just looked at him.

"Oh, that Walter," he said with trepidation. "Let's talk about this right here. I don't want your mother to hear any of this. Okay, what happened". Al told him the story about recognizing Walter as the boyfriend of a murder victim when he came in to be interviewed and that she wasn't sure if Walter had seen her. She told him how powerful and rich that Robert Whittington had become since their encounter in 2006, and how she had been tasked with looking into his background.

"If you try to arrest him for anything, then he will expose what I did, mija," mumbled Bennie. "He's paid us in advance for our silence. I feared this day would come," said Al. "I don't know how he's involved in his daughter's murder or the body found in his business two years ago, but I think that he's capable of anything. I could tell that he was an evil man from the day that we met him. What should I do papa?"

"Do your job," Bennie replied. "I knew that I would have to pay for what I did sooner or later. I guess pay day is here. Do the right thing baby girl. I am so sorry for compromising you and now you have to do what I should have done a long time ago.  Do what is honest and right."

Al and Logan briefed Marcus, Lieutenant O'Malley and Sergeant U on what they had found and they all devised a plan.  Logan and Al were to set up surveillance on Walter Chase.  They wanted to know where his daily travels took him and with whom he associated with besides Robert Whittington.  The Homicide Division had a black van that they used for these kinds of operations. They were prepared to start the surveillance the next morning at Walter Chase's home in Bethesda, Maryland. They met at zero three hundred hours in front of the Homicide Division to pick up the van.

They were both dressed casually.  Detective Alverez wore a tight pair of jeans and a form fitting shirt. Logan looked at her and said, "damn Al, how am I supposed to concentrate with you looking like that?" Detective Alverez laughed and said, "you have a one track mind.  Is that all you think about Logan?" "Unfortunately yes, most of the time," he replied. "But listen, I understand where you're coming from and I promise to be professional.  I really like you and I don't want to do anything to compromise your position here. I apologize for being a man," he joked.

"Are you giving me your word Logan," she asked. "Yep, word is bond," said Logan.  "You are so juvenile," she joked, "but I appreciate it."  Logan looked her in the eye and said, "but you do know that every once in a while, I'm gonna look at your ass," as he grinned. "If that's all you do is look, I can handle that," she said with a smile.

"Let's make sure that we have everything before we get started. I hope Marcus trained you right," she joked. "I've got the water, binoculars, cell phone, camera, sandwiches, a few snacks and my trusty slap jack." A slap jack was a leather case about six inches long with a handle on one end and a round piece of steel inside of the other end. It was small enough to be concealed in his back pocket and lethal enough to knock the shit out of anyone. "And last but not least, my baby (as he patted his glock holstered on his right side)."

"I see that Marcus has taught you well," said Al, but you do know that it's against department regulations to carry that slap jack?" "What slap jack," he replied, "and you know I was a detective before I came to homicide" said Logan. "We did surveillance operations all the time." "Point taken, you might actually know what you're doing," Al replied.

They parked a few houses down from Walter's house and saw him walk out and get into his black Audi. They followed him to a real estate company in Rockville, Maryland. Another dummy corporation for Robert Whittington. As they waited for him to come back out, Logan said to Al, "is something wrong, you seem like your mind is somewhere else?" Al looked intensely at Logan and asked, "it's about the job, can I trust you?"

Her question surprised him and being a veteran of the police department, he knew exactly what that meant. It meant that she had a secret that few people knew about and that secret could possibly cost her job. Knowing her secret could also jeopardize his job. If it was about something illegal, he was bound by the police department general orders and the D.C. Code to report it. If he didn't, he could be breaking the law. But Logan was what they called, "a stand up guy". If he gave his word, he would take your secret to the grave. "Yes Al," as he nodded his head, "you can trust me."

She started off, "let me tell you a hypothetical story. In 2006, there was this rookie officer that responded to a burglar alarm in Georgetown. She found the back door open so she called for K-9 to search the building. Once the building was cleared, this officer observed her partner take money out of a safe and put it in his pocket. The officer kept silent and told no one. A few months later, the two officers were contacted by an employee of the business where the money was taken from and asked to meet with the owner."

"The owner showed them both a tape of the one officer observing the other officer take the money. The owner basically told them that he could either report them to Internal Affairs or they could keep the money and would owe him a favor in the future. They chose the latter." "Wow, let me guess...it's time to return that favor," Logan asked? "It could be," she replied. "The employee that contacted the officers and observed that meeting is Walter Chase. The owner of the business is Robert Whittington," said Al. "So, have they asked for anything yet," Logan inquired? "Not yet, but if we find something to arrest one or both of them for, I'm sure that the past will rear its ugly head."

An hour later, Walter Chase walks out of that business with a brief case in hand. He gets into his car and drives to a payday loan office in Maryland. After an hour passes, he exits again, still with the brief case in hand and drives to several more payday loan establishments in D.C. "Every place that ole Walter has visited is a company that is co-owned by Robert Whittington," Logan noted. "All these addresses came up in our checks of Robert Whittington yesterday," he added. "I wonder what's in the brief case." This cycle of going in and out of these types businesses went on into the night.

It was really late and Walter's last stop was at a small night club/bar in Northeast, D.C. After an hour and a half passed and there was no sign of Walter, Logan went inside of the bar to see what he was doing and to make sure that he hadn't given them the slip, while Al stayed in the car. After ten minutes, Al got impatient and walked around to the back of the establishment to see if there was a back door. As she got to the back,

Walter exits out of the rear door and is surprised to see her. "Officer Alverez, it's a pleasure to see you again." "It's Detective Alverez now," she replied. "Glad to see that your past hasn't effected your career," as he grinned sarcastically.

He suspiciously switches the brief case from his left hand to his right hand. "What's in the brief case Walter," she asks? "I'm gonna need you to go away and to forget that you saw me," says Walter with an angry scowl on his face. "Can't do it Walter," said Al as she places her right hand on her gun affixed to her waist.

"Listen, I'm in a hurry and I don't have time for this. You owe us a favor and now it's time to pay it back. GO AWAY!" "Or what," Al asked? Walter then grabs Al's right hand to prevent her from drawing her weapon. He drops the brief case and grabs Al in the front of her throat with his other hand. He pushed her back into a brick wall, while choking her. Al struggles to break free but can't escape his grasp. "Detective, we had an agreement, don't make me hurt you." Al struggles to break free as she gasped for air.

Just then Logan grabbed Walter around his neck in a choke hold, "damn Walter, still beating up women," he asked? Logan backed up while maintaining his grip around Walter's neck at which time Walter released his hold on Al. As Al moved away, Logan pushed Walter forward, "place your hands on the wall, time to go to jail Walt." Walter placed both hands on the wall and Al reached into Walter's rear waistband and removed a hand gun. "You got a permit for this" she asked? "As a matter of fact, I do. Look inside my wallet in my back pants pocket."

Al removed his wallet and located Walter's permit to carry a concealed weapon. "What business are you in that you need to carry a concealed weapon," Al asked? "LAWYER," he replied. "But I don't think that you really want me to go to jail and be questioned about the things that I know, cause I've got stories to tell."

"Fuck your threats," said Logan. "If my partner gives me the nod, you're going to jail for assaulting a police officer," as Logan looked at Al. Al looked at Logan and nodded affirmative, "we're putting his ass on the books" (arrest book) she said. Walter then quickly pushed himself off the wall and spun around. He stepped to the side and got into a karate stance. "You've got to be kidding me," said Logan, as he put his hands up in a fighting stance. Walter attempted to kick Logan in the right side of his head with his left foot, which Logan blocked. "You know a little something, huh," said Logan, as he punched Walter right in the nose, sending blood gushing out. Walter yelled in frustration as he charged Logan, pushing him back. Al then struck Walter in his right temple with her slap jack, knocking him out as he fell to the ground with a thud.

"Meet Pedro, mutha fucker," referring to her slap jack. "You're not the only one who carries one of these," she said while looking at Pedro. Then she placed it back into her rear pocket. Logan handcuffed Walter and called for an ambulance to transport him to the hospital. Al laid Walter's briefcase flat on the ground and opened it. Both there eyes lit up as it was full of one hundred dollar bills. "He was either making collections or distributing this money to be laundered. Either way, we'll find out later," said Logan. They placed all of the money on the evidence books and Walter was arrested for Assault on a Police Officer. While at the police station, Logan said to Al, "you know I didn't need your help with Walter. I can kick his ass any day." "I know," she responded, "but I needed yours. Thanks."

# Chapter Fourteen
## Her Dirty Little Secret

The next morning as usual, the squad has roll call at zero six hundred hours. Marcus briefs the lieutenant on his progress: "I don't believe that Walter Chase or Robert Whittington have anything to do with Laura Whittington's death. Their crimes involve money laundering among other things. Detective Alverez is meeting with Laura Whittington's best friend at Haines Point at ten hundred hours this morning. Her name is Kristina Blanco and she knows the identity of the ex-boyfriend and she also believes that he had motive to kill her. Al's gonna get all the info we need this morning." "Sounds like he's our man. Great," the lieutenant responds.

Detective Alverez do you need any assistance from the squad" the lieutenant asks? "No sir. It's routine. I'll get this scum bags identity and then we can all go lock his ass up." "Great, keep me informed" replied the lieutenant as he walks back to his office. Marcus asks Al, "What's the deal on Ms. Blanco?" "She's supposed to meet me at the south end of Haines Point in the parking lot by the bathrooms. She'll be driving a red Jetta. I'll get all the info on the ex and we'll close this case out." "Thanks Al."

"Ray, did you submit the DNA samples," Marcus asks? "Yep, they will notify me when any results come in." "Ok, great. Let's all meet back here at fourteen hundred hours to track down the ex-boyfriend. I'm ready to put this case to a close."

At zero nine thirty hours, Kristina Blanco's red Jetta with heavily tinted windows was parked by the bathrooms in Haines Point. Detective Ray Barlow walks up to the vehicle with his gun in his left hand and quickly opens the driver's side door. He's surprised to see it's empty. Just then Marcus and Logan walk out of the bathroom near Kristina's vehicle. Al and Big Russ emerge from the wood line and Lieutenant O'Malley and Sergeant U quickly drive up. "Ray, what are you doing here and why is your gun out," Marcus asks? "Uh...I uh...was coming to back Alverez up. I didn't want her meeting the girlfriend by herself," he responded as he quickly holsters his weapon. "Ray...you killed her, didn't you," Marcus asks? "Killed who, Kristina Blanco," he responded? "No, Laura Whittington," said Marcus. "What would make you think something crazy like that," as Ray lets out a nervous laugh.

"It took me a while, but I figured it out Ray. I was a little suspicious on the very first day at the crime scene. The rest of the squad had been there for hours and we were discussing the scene. You had just arrived and before walking around the house you were able to tell us that the upstairs windows were not alarmed. How would you know that unless you had been here before and were very familiar with the home," Marcus explained.

"That's not enough for you to accuse me of murder," Ray exclaimed. "There's more Ray. You were supposed to do a canvass of Laura Whittington's neighbors to see if any of them had security cameras that viewed the alley or the rear of Laura Whittington's house. You said that none of them did. Logan checked and found that two of the neighbors had cameras that captured a tall male entering her back yard before the murder and exiting after the murder. The images did not capture the face, but the body type matched you and Walter Chase. The two of you have a similar build." Ray shook his head "it wasn't me."

"I'm not finished Ray," as Marcus reluctantly continued. "There was a DNA sample taken from Laura Whittington's fingernails. You said that you submitted the sample but that wasn't true. I checked and it was never submitted. Of course I submitted it later and when the results come back, I'm sure that it will match your DNA. Which also explains the scratches that we all saw on your arms the day after the murder when you entered roll call, late again."

"By your own admission, you said that it came from a screamer. Did Laura Whittington scream when you killed her?" "Yeah I said it, but I didn't mean Laura Whittington," as Ray continued to deny the truth.

Marcus continued, "and then there's Kristina Blanco. Laura Whittington's best friend. Al actually interviewed her early this morning before roll call and she had some very interesting insight. She told us about Laura's ex-boyfriend. She never met him and didn't know his name, but she knew all about him."

"Most importantly, she knew that Laura Whittington ended their relationship because of his profession and the fact that his profession was financially beneath her family's standards. He was a cop Ray. And not just any kind of cop, he was a detective. Last but not least, about six months ago, you told Logan about this rich chick that you were dating and had fallen in love with and how she ended the relationship. All the evidence points to Laura Whittington being that woman and you being the person that killed her."

Ray paused and sighed. He looked up, then down and then at each member of the squad, wondering how they viewed him. What did they think of him now? "Come on man," Marcus pleaded. "You gotta come clean, that's the only way that we can help you." Ray looked at Marcus and shook his head "we both know that you can't help me. There ain't a damn thing you can do for me now."

"Yeah, Laura and I dated for about six months and everything was fine until her daddy got involved. Suddenly, I wasn't good enough for her and we shouldn't be together. Then I became her dirty little secret. I even had to park a few blocks away and come in through the back door with a key that she gave me. She didn't want anyone to see me."

"At first the sneaking around was exciting, but then it became degrading. I wasn't good enough for her, didn't make enough money, didn't have enough class." He laughed as he continued, "then one night she tells me that it's over. Talkin 'bout she thought that it was best if we saw other people. That bitch thinks she can kick me to the curb and replace me with that pretty boy Walter."

"Who does that," he asks indignantly? The members of the squad are shocked as they listen to Ray's rant. Ray continues, "I would call her sometimes 'cause I wanted to convince her to change her mind. I'm the man for her...not him. Then she stopped taking my calls, wouldn't answer the damn phone. I can just see her now, looking at the caller ID, knowing that it's me and still not answering. I deserved better than that. I was good to her. I loved her! I still had my key, so I went over there that morning. Just to talk to her. Just to convince her to take me back."

"I used my key and came in through the back door and I see her in the kitchen. She had the nerve to be mad that I used the key that she gave me. If she didn't want me to use it then she should have changed the damn lock" as Ray's tone gets louder in obvious agitation. The squad continues to listen in amazement.

"She wouldn't listen to me and tries to walk away and dismiss me.  Says she'll call the police if I don't leave." "Please," he says with disgust "call the police on me.  I am the fucking police."

"I grabbed her from behind and she started to flail her arms and tried to get away.  I just wanted to stop her from calling the police on me.  I grabbed her and held her tight, just trying to stop her.  I just held her tightly and then all of a sudden, she stopped moving and slumped in my arms.  I checked her pulse and she was dead.  It was an accident.  I was just trying to make her listen.  I was scared and I panicked.  I went upstairs and got the gun that she kept in her night stand.  I struggled to pick her up with my right arm and shot her in the head to make it seem like she killed herself."

A tear trickled down Ray's face.  "After that, it all got fuzzy.  I dropped the gun and used the computer in her office to type a suicide note.  I didn't mean to kill her."  By now, Logan was standing next to Ray.  Logan gently removed Ray's gun from his holster and handed it to Sergeant U.  Ray turned and hugged his old friend Logan and broke down in tears.  The realization of what he had done and the bleak outlook for his future was too much for Ray to handle.  He sobbed in Logan's arms like a baby before being arrested and taken to the station for processing.

After Ray was processed, Marcus, Logan and Big Russ sat at their desks in quiet reflection, pondering the events of the day. Detective Katelyn Alverez walks out of Lieutenant O'Malley's office with Sergeant U. "I know that was hard for you but you did the right thing," said Sergeant U as he gives her a hug.

Detective Alverez walked over to Logan "I told the lieutenant about my past indiscretion and gave him my gun and badge. He says that Internal Affairs will investigate and he put me on administrative leave until its conclusion." Marcus gave her a confused look. "It's a long story Marcus, but I give Logan my blessing to tell you all about it," as she kissed Logan on the cheek. "Hasta luego," she said before walking away and as usual, Logan stared at her ass as she left the squad room.

The events of the day took a lot out of Marcus. Finding out that the murderer he'd been chasing was not only a member of his police department, but also a member of his squad was mind boggling. It drained him mentally to the point that he needed to take a few days off to re-charge his battery. As he drove home, he reflected on the years that he worked with Ray and couldn't help but think that he should have seen signs that he was capable of such a heinous crime. He thought about the fact that two lives had been lost. Laura's and Ray's. After years of being the murder police, he thought that he'd seen everything. Very little surprised him...until now and his disappointment was obvious.

Marcus took pride in having a balanced life. When his work life weighed him down, it was time to submerge himself into his family and Gina was his stabilizer. As Marcus opened his front door, he was greeted by Gina. She knew him well and could see by the look on his face that something was wrong. "You okay babe" she asked? Marcus just shook his head, no. "You wouldn't believe my day babe," he said as they embraced. "Dinner will be ready soon and the kids are at your mom's for the weekend." Marcus locked the front door and kicked off his shoes. He walked to his bedroom, removed his gun and put it in his nightstand, then locked the drawer. He took off his department issued cell phone and turned it off. Took off his suit and tie and changed into a pair of sweats and a t-shirt. He took a seat at the kitchen counter as Gina finished preparing their meal. Marcus looked into Gina's eyes and said "I love you." She blushed and said, "I love you too baby, tell me about your day."

Anthony D. White was born in Washington D.C., raised in D.C. and neighboring Maryland. He moved to Virginia as an adult and therefore claims what we affectionately call the DMV (DC, Maryland, Virginia) as home. He is married and has two adult children. In addition, he has traveled the world, serving our country as a member of the United States Air Force and is presently a twenty four year member of the Metropolitan Police Department of Washington D.C.

This is A.D.White's first Murder Mystery. He has previously written three books of Erotic Fiction under the pen name of Blaine Barlow.
www.blainebarlow.com

Your feedback is greatly appreciated. Please leave a comment about the book at his website,
www.adwhite.net

Editors:

Dolores W. Allen
Rosalind N. White
Brenda D. Woodson

Cover Art Designed by Colette Butfiloski

Consultant: Detective First Class Darryl Richmond Sr.
            Metropolitan Police Department
            Washington, D.C.

Made in the USA
Middletown, DE
29 June 2021

43164477R00075